MANHUNT

ALSO BY
KATE MESSNER

THE SILVER JAGUAR SOCIETY MYSTERIES
Capture the Flag
Hide and Seek

OTHER NOVELS
The Brilliant Fall of Gianna Z.
Eye of the Storm
Sugar and Ice
Wake Up Missing

THE MARTY MCGUIRE SERIES
Marty McGuire
Marty McGuire Digs Worms!
Marty McGuire Has Too Many Pets!

PICTURE BOOKS
Over and Under the Snow
Sea Monster's First Day
Sea Monster and the Bossy Fish

MANHUNT

KATE MESSNER

SCHOLASTIC PRESS / NEW YORK

Copyright © 2014 by Kate Messner

Library of Congress Cataloging-in-Publication Data

Messner, Kate, author.
Manhunt / by Kate Messner. — First edition.
pages cm
Summary: Henry, Anna, and José, the junior members of the Silver Jaguar Society, are on a mission in Paris to recover the *Mona Lisa* — but when senior members of the society are taken hostage, it is up to Henry to rescue them while continuing to pursue the missing masterpiece.
1. Art thefts — Juvenile fiction. 2. Hostages — Juvenile fiction. 3. Secret societies — Juvenile fiction. 4. Adventure stories. 5. Paris (France) — Juvenile fiction. [1. Art thefts — Fiction. 2. Hostages — Fiction. 3. Secret societies — Fiction. 4. Adventure and adventurers — Fiction. 5. Paris (France) — Fiction. 6. France — Fiction.] I. Title.
PZ7.M5615Man 2014
[Fic] — dc23
2013030242

ISBN 978-0-545-41977-2
10 9 8 7 6 5 4 3 2 1   14 15 16 17 18
Printed in the U.S.A.   23
First edition, July 2014

Title page character illustrations copyright © 2014 by Yuta Onoda
Interior illustrations copyright © 2014 by Whitney Lyle
Author's note photographs by Kate Messner
Book design by Whitney Lyle

FOR LINDSAY, STEVEN,
AND BRENDAN

ONE

Breaking glass and wailing alarm bells shattered the midnight quiet just before Henry Thorn's baby sister was born.

Dressed in black and cloaked in shadows, thieves rappelled up a wall of the Tokyo National Museum, burst through a high window, and ripped Hasegawa Tōhaku's ghostly painting of pine trees from the wall.

When midnight came to Shanghai an hour later, a man in a museum security guard uniform raised a hammer to the glass case before him, swung hard, and snatched the polished jade dragon sculpture that rested inside. The jagged glass caught his sleeve, and he left a trail of blood all through the antiquities wing as alarms echoed off the walls.

Five hours later, the people of Saint Petersburg, Russia, woke to sirens, but it was already too late. No one knows how the thieves entered, but museum cameras caught them racing off with a bouquet of flowers made entirely from precious metals and gemstones.

Masterpieces fell like dominoes as midnight raced around the globe.

In Oslo, someone stole *The Scream*. Edvard Munch's haunting image of a melting face stared aghast from its canvas as it was carried out the museum's back door into the night.

In Florence, a man dressed as a janitor put down his mop, pulled a razor blade from his pocket, and sliced *The Birth of Venus* from its frame.

In Amsterdam, the target was *The Night Watch*, Rembrandt's famous painting of a militia preparing to go out on patrol. Thieves carefully cut the canvas from its frame, rolled it up, and ran off with it, right under the painted militiamen's own watchful noses.

In Paris, a dozen thugs swarmed the Louvre, plucking paintings from the walls with practiced hands.

Rembrandt. Monet. Da Vinci.

Gone.

In Madrid, five enormous men wrenched *The Garden of Earthly Delights* from the wall, folded up its three panels, and walked it out the door as if it weighed no more than a gift shop poster. They roared off in a dark blue van before police cars even arrived on the block.

But the authorities did show up eventually, at all those museums in all those cities. When they saw the smashed cases and vacant frames, when they realized the scope of the crimes, how they'd spread around the world like a pandemic, phones began to ring. Phones at police stations and investigators' homes. Phones in international agency headquarters and museum executive offices.

A phone rang at Henry's house, too.

It was past midnight. He'd given up on sleep but was in bed playing his SuperGamePrism-5000 when he heard Aunt Lucinda answer.

"Hello?" A pause. "What's happening?" Her voice was full of worry.

Henry's stomach tightened. He climbed out of bed and hurried to the kitchen. "Is it Dad?"

Aunt Lucinda held up a finger.

Henry's dad and stepmom, Bethany, had rushed to the hospital during dinner when it looked like Bethany might be ready to have her baby. Aunt Lucinda had hurried over from her apartment down the block to stay with Henry. The baby wasn't due for another month and a half, so they'd been waiting all night for the phone to ring, hoping everything was okay.

"So who's there now?" Aunt Lucinda asked the person on the other end. She looked up at the clock.

"Why didn't they alert us sooner? We could have —"
She stopped. "I know." And sighed.

Henry went to the refrigerator and poured himself
a glass of milk. He wasn't thirsty, but he needed to do
something. Whatever was going on sounded bad.

"All right. I'll be there in the morning." Aunt
Lucinda set her phone down and looked at Henry,
who put down his milk.

"Did she have the baby? Is everything okay?"

"That wasn't your dad," Aunt Lucinda said, opening her laptop on the table. "I'm sure he and Bethany
are fine and still waiting, or we would have heard."

"Oh!" The bad news hadn't come from the hospital. "Then what —"

"Shh!" Aunt Lucinda's fingers flew over her keyboard. She hunched over the screen, squinting at
search results.

"Aunt Lucinda, what's going on?"

She leaned back in her chair, looking out the
window into the night. "Someone targeted a dozen
museums all over the world tonight, Henry. They
made off with works of art that will probably be gone
forever unless we find them soon."

"*We?*" Henry asked.

Aunt Lucinda nodded. "The Silver Jaguar Society
has called an emergency meeting at its headquarters
here in Boston tomorrow."

TWO

Technically, Henry was only a junior Silver Jaguar Society member, an honor bestowed on him after he and two other kids — Anna Revere-Hobbs and José McGilligan — had solved the mystery of the stolen Star-Spangled Banner in Washington, DC, last winter. Before that, Henry hadn't known there even *was* a Silver Jaguar Society.

But now he knew that his mom had been part of the society until she died of cancer four years ago. Like all the other members, she'd taken an oath and promised to do everything in her power to protect the world's artifacts.

He knew that Aunt Lucinda's frequent trips were actually secret missions. And he'd learned about the society's archnemesis — Vincent Goosen, the ring-leader of an international art-theft gang called the

Serpentine Princes, responsible for some of the biggest art heists in history.

Henry had encountered Goosen back in June when he and Anna and José were in Costa Rica while their parents investigated the disappearance of a society artifact called the Jaguar Cup. The kids had been staying at a rain forest lodge, supposedly out of danger, when they'd come face-to-face with Goosen and another former Serpentine Prince. Goosen's mean black eyes and his greasy mustache still gave Henry nightmares sometimes — so now, with his mind full of late-night secrets and stolen art, sleep was even harder to come by.

In the morning, Henry woke to another ringing phone, but by the time he got to the kitchen, Aunt Lucinda was already hanging up.

"That was your dad," she announced, tossing Henry a banana, "and you are officially a big brother! Kara Akita Thorn was born a little after three this morning."

"Oh!" Henry felt the heaviness of his tossing, turning night start to lift. "Everything's okay?"

Aunt Lucinda nodded. "The baby was early. She's getting special care, but she'll be fine."

"That's great." Henry set the banana on the table. He wasn't awake enough to eat. "When are they coming home?"

"Not for a while. The baby has to be watched

closely for a few days, so your dad and Bethany will stay at the hospital for now, too. They can't bear to leave her."

"Oh. Okay." They didn't seem to have any trouble leaving Henry, but if he mentioned that, he'd probably get that lecture he'd already heard a thousand times. *Babies need lots of attention. We're counting on you to be more independent. Blah blah blah.* Henry picked up the banana and gave it a squeeze. The peel split, and a glob of banana mush plopped onto the wood floor.

"Stop that," Aunt Lucinda said, "and eat your breakfast so we can go. I have to make a stop before the meeting this morning."

· • ◉ • ·

Aunt Lucinda's stop turned out to be a seriously fancy-pants museum. "I can't believe I've never brought you here," she said as they walked up to the big wooden door. The museum was closed, but Aunt Lucinda flashed her identification, and two guards let them in. "The Isabella Stewart Gardner Museum is my favorite." She sighed. "It's sad you won't get to see her."

"Is she out of town or something?" Henry looked around at the chandeliers and sculptures.

"Oh, no. She's been dead for nearly a hundred years," Aunt Lucinda said, leading Henry upstairs and through a room full of paintings.

"I'm pretty sure I don't need to see her, then."

"I wasn't talking about seeing her in person," Aunt Lucinda said, turning a corner. "I was talking about this." She pointed to a plain brown frame that seemed to be showing off the wallpaper behind it.

Aunt Lucinda was getting weirder by the minute, Henry decided. "Is that, like, her ghost?"

"It was her portrait, Henry. Until last night." Aunt Lucinda rummaged through her purse, pulled out a museum brochure, and opened it to a painting of a tall lady in a black dress.

"She used to be in here?" Henry pointed to the empty frame.

Aunt Lucinda nodded and blinked her teary eyes. "I used to come stand in front of her when I felt like I needed wisdom or strength for a society mission." She looked around quickly, then lowered her voice. "She was one of us, you know."

"Oh!" Henry looked more closely at the lady in the brochure painting. Her eyes looked worried, as if she'd known all those years ago she might be stolen some day.

"There you are! I am so sorry to be late." A skinny Asian man with wispy black hair hurried up to them and hugged Aunt Lucinda.

"The portrait was the only loss?" she asked him.

"It was." He shook his head. "It happened so fast, almost as if they knew they'd only have time to get one piece."

"And they chose her," Aunt Lucinda said, biting her lip.

"It's a stunning portrait," the man said, looking through the frame at the wallpaper. "Though not the most valuable. Our Dutch masters weren't touched this time."

"Thank goodness," Aunt Lucinda said.

Henry frowned. "What do you mean, 'this time'?"

Aunt Lucinda pursed her lips. "Thieves dressed as Boston police officers made off with a number of priceless paintings back in 1990," she said, "including two Rembrandts and a Vermeer." She looked at the Asian man. "I fear Mrs. Stewart Gardner has gone to join them."

He nodded sadly. "Perhaps this time, we'll have more luck finding the stolen art."

"Thank you, David," Aunt Lucinda said, then turned to Henry. "We should get going."

The whole cab ride, Aunt Lucinda bit her lip and stared out the window, while Henry wondered where they'd have the big Silver Jaguar Society meeting. Probably some fancy hotel or office building. Maybe they'd have those big soft leather seats that spun around.

Or not. The taxi stopped at Big Al's North End Pizza.

Aunt Lucinda thanked the driver, paid, and got out. "Let's go. We're already late."

Henry climbed out of the cab and stared. The place was a total dive. Even the neon sign outside looked greasy. "Silver Jaguar Society headquarters is a *pizza* place?"

"No, Henry," Aunt Lucinda said, opening the door. "The society's *cover* is a pizza place." She waved to a kid tossing a circle of dough in the air behind the counter, then followed a narrow hallway past the restrooms to a door marked STORAGE. She turned the jiggly doorknob and pulled it open to reveal a set of old stone steps. "Our Boston headquarters is downstairs."

THREE

"Henry!"

"You're here!"

Anna Revere-Hobbs and José McGilligan jumped up from a small table littered with books and playing cards. Anna ran at Henry and hugged him so hard she almost knocked him into Aunt Lucinda.

"Hey! You don't have to tackle me."

"Sorry." Anna stepped back. "We didn't know if you'd be able to come, with the new baby and all. My mom told us what's going on. I hope everything's okay."

"Me too." José shook Henry's hand, then pointed to the third chair at their rickety table. "We've been hanging out here. You want to play cards?"

"You do that," Aunt Lucinda said, already heading for a shiny steel door across the room.

"But I thought we had that meeting."

"The *adults* are meeting in here." Aunt Lucinda tapped the door. "*Your* meeting is here." She pointed at the crummy table and chairs.

"Wait . . ." Henry didn't even like cards. "Shouldn't we check in with Dad at the hospital first? How long's your meeting going to last?"

"It's hard to say. I'll touch base with your dad and get an update in a little while." Aunt Lucinda punched some numbers into a keypad and pulled open the door.

Henry tried to see inside the big room, but all he caught was a glimpse of long tables and clusters of people and computer workstations before the door slammed shut.

"They won't let us in," Anna said. "I tried. But there's a heating duct or something under the table. José and I have been taking turns listening."

José held up his pointer finger. "Shakespeare said, 'Listen to many. Speak to a few.'"

José was big on quoting famous guys. He said it gave him inspiration and helped him think better. It was also incredibly annoying.

"Yeah, well . . . I bet Shakespeare got to listen somewhere better than a dumb pizza place basement." But Henry crawled under the table and tipped his ear to the grate.

"Anything?" Anna called from above.

"Nah. It's quiet. But what have you heard?" Henry asked. "Do they think Vincent Goosen is behind all the heists?"

"Totally," Anna said. "And they're worried that somebody *inside* the society is feeding information to the Serpentine Princes."

"A traitor?" Henry looked out from under the table. "Should they even be talking in there if somebody's leaking information?"

"They don't seem worried about the people here right now. Come on up and I'll show you what we know so far."

Anna opened her notebook while Henry slid into a chair. "The thefts all happened at midnight, all around the world. I heard my mom talking on the phone after she thought I had gone to bed, and I put together this chart."

Anna turned to a page where she'd drawn a rough world map. It was covered in notes, and she'd sketched in pictures of famous works of art, floating around in the oceans. Arrows pointed from the art to a dozen different cities.

Henry leaned closer and saw that each city was also labeled with the name of a museum and notes about what was stolen from it.

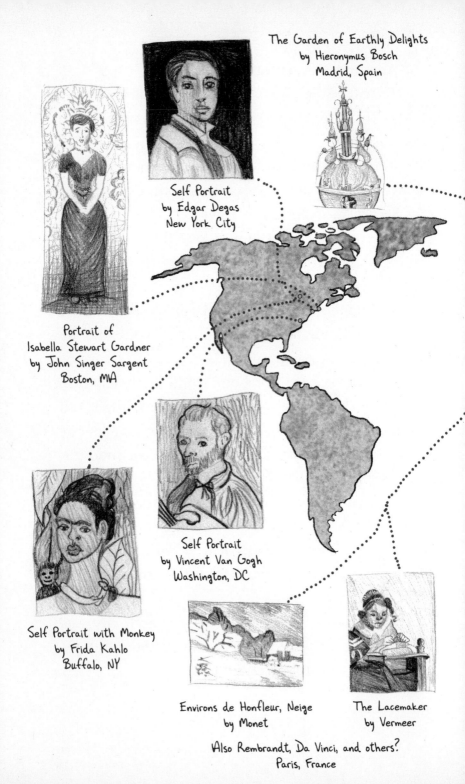

The Garden of Earthly Delights
by Hieronymus Bosch
Madrid, Spain

Self Portrait
by Edgar Degas
New York City

Portrait of
Isabella Stewart Gardner
by John Singer Sargent
Boston, MA

Self Portrait
by Vincent Van Gogh
Washington, DC

Self Portrait with Monkey
by Frida Kahlo
Buffalo, NY

Environs de Honfleur, Neige
by Monet

The Lacemaker
by Vermeer

Also Rembrandt, Da Vinci, and others?
Paris, France

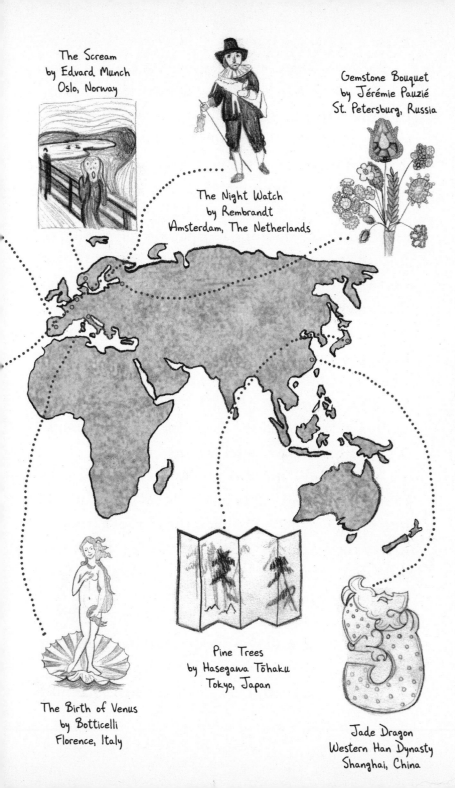

The Scream
by Edvard Munch
Oslo, Norway

The Night Watch
by Rembrandt
Amsterdam, The Netherlands

Gemstone Bouquet
by Jérémie Pauzié
St. Petersburg, Russia

The Birth of Venus
by Botticelli
Florence, Italy

Pine Trees
by Hasegawa Tōhaku
Tokyo, Japan

Jade Dragon
Western Han Dynasty
Shanghai, China

Henry looked at it, then tipped back in his chair. "Dude, can you imagine how many people it must have taken to pull this off?"

"It's impressive," José said, "but I can't help wondering why they chose staggered times."

"Wasn't it all at midnight?" Henry asked.

"Yeah, but midnight doesn't happen everywhere at once," José said, pointing to Japan on the map. "The first theft happened at midnight in Tokyo. It was eleven in the morning here in Boston when that happened, then noon when they got the jade dragon in Shanghai, dinnertime when they broke into the European museums, and midnight — *our* midnight — when they hit Boston, Buffalo, and New York."

"That's weird," Henry said. "Wouldn't the earlier thefts kind of sound the alarm for other museums? Whoever did this was kind of stupid."

"Or so brilliant they knew they wouldn't be caught." José frowned thoughtfully. "What if they did it to make a point? Midnight is the start of a new day. Maybe the Serpentine Princes wanted to send a message that things are going to be different . . . that they're going to call the shots from now on?"

"Goosen was furious when his mansion in Amsterdam got raided. They were talking about that earlier." Anna tipped her head toward the meeting room. "The society thinks Goosen might be planning to use the stolen art as leverage so the authorities will release his son."

"Oh, yeah. I forgot his son was in prison," Henry said. When Goosen and his grown son were arrested in the raid, Goosen had escaped within days, but his kid was still behind bars.

"Did they say anything about Goosen's other son?" José asked. "The one who supposedly went missing a few years ago?"

"Not that I heard, but the society thinks — wait . . . are they talking again?" Anna pushed her chair back, crawled under the table, and put her ear to the grate. After a few minutes, she scrambled back out from under the table. "Okay, this is good! I couldn't hear everything, but it sounds like they're going to have the members split up and head to all the cities where museums got hit. And somebody — maybe your aunt, Henry — said something about looking for her in the tunnels!"

Anna looked all excited, but Henry didn't get it. "What tunnels? And who is *her*?"

"A piece of stolen art, I bet," Anna said. "One of the paintings or sculptures must be hidden in a tunnel!"

"Maybe," José said. "I suppose some of them were portraits of women."

"Hey! It could be that lady from the Gardner museum," Henry said.

"Oh! Isabella Stewart Gardner! My mom told me about that." Anna pulled out her notebook and started scribbling. "Okay . . . now tunnels . . . where are there tunnels in Boston?"

"There are subway tunnels, right?" José turned to Henry. "You're the one who lives here. Anything else?"

"I don't know. It's not like —" But Henry stopped. He did know about some tunnels. "Actually, yeah! When my class went to the Old North Church on a field trip, the tour guide said smugglers and pirates used tunnels around there to hide stuff from the British in the old days."

"Ohmygosh, this is so perfect!" Anna started shoving her notebook and papers into her backpack. "I saw signs for that church on the way here. I bet it's close, and it's not like we have anything else to do."

"Yeah, but . . ." José pointed to the door to the meeting room. "If they know where she's hidden — whoever *she* is — why don't *they* go get her?"

"Because grown-ups love meetings — that's why." Henry was already bored with this one. "They'll be in there talking for hours before they get around to doing anything. Dude, if we find the painting ourselves, we can prop old Isabella up against the wall and have her standing here in her black dress to greet 'em when they finally open the door." Henry smiled, just thinking about it. "I say we go check this out."

FOUR

Henry left a note on the table in case the grown-ups finished their meeting, even though that didn't seem likely to happen any time soon.

Gone for a walk to see historical sites. Back by noon.

When Henry and José got upstairs, Anna was handing money to the guy behind the pizza counter. "Here," she said, handing out paper plates with greasy slices spilling over the edges. "It's early for pizza, but I know how you guys are, and I don't want to have to stop and go looking for muffins or something once we get started."

A muffin would have been awesome, Henry thought. With his dad stuck at the hospital and Aunt Lucinda caught up in her society stuff, he'd only had that half-smooshed banana for breakfast. But there were no muffins, so he ate his crummy pizza as they walked down the street, shuffling through crunchy fallen leaves. "I think that church is around the corner."

Anna ran ahead. "I see it!" She opened her notebook while Henry and José caught up. "Okay, Henry, tell us what you know."

"Uh, well . . . the Old North Church is where they hung the lanterns before Paul Revere's ride to warn everybody the redcoats were coming," Henry explained. "You know . . . one if by land and two if by —"

"I know *that* part. I mean, hello? One of my last names is Revere."

"Oh. Right." Henry did know that. Everyone in the Silver Jaguar Society had a famous ancestor who was an artist or creator or inventor. Henry was the descendent of Grace Wisher, an indentured servant who helped create the original Star-Spangled Banner. José was related to a Mexican artist lady named Friday or Frito — Henry never got her name right. And Anna's great-great-something-or-other was Paul Revere.

Henry shrugged. "I don't know any more about the tunnels. We can ask inside."

They crossed the narrow street to the church and looked up at its old brick tower.

"Finish that pizza," Anna said, heading for the door. "I doubt you can bring food in the church."

Henry folded the rest of his pizza slice in half, then in half again, and shoved it in his mouth so his cheeks bulged out.

"Nice." Anna looked at him, shaking her head. "Very nice."

Henry tried to say, "I need energy to investigate," but it came out as "Oo-noo-oo-noo-doo-to-enoodogah." He followed Anna and José inside.

A short-haired woman wearing red-framed glasses and a dark blue golf shirt greeted them. "You're just in time. Come with me and you can join the tour." She led them to the front of the church where some old people were already gathered.

"Welcome to the Old North Church, built in 1723 and famous for its role in Paul Revere's midnight ride. But we're full of all kinds of history." The guide pointed toward the back of the church. "Note the angel sculptures in our choir loft." Four carved angels perched on podiums around the organ's golden pipes as if they were standing guard.

"They're lovely," one of the old ladies said.

"They're stolen," said the tour guide.

"Awesome!" said Henry. The guide on his school trip hadn't mentioned that.

"These angels were on a French ship bound for Quebec when the vessel was captured by pirates in 1746," the guide said. "They unpacked the ship's cargo here in Boston, hid the loot, and —"

"In tunnels?" Anna blurted out.

"Quite possibly." The tour guide looked impressed. "Our Old North End is riddled with tunnels that were used by pirates and smugglers. And then the pirates donated these angels to the Old North Church. Now . . ."

Anna raised her hand. "Are there tunnels near here?"

The woman frowned. "Yes, but they're closed off. Now, if you'll follow me . . ."

Anna waved her hand wildly.

"Yes?"

"Where exactly are those closed-off tunnels?"

"There's an entrance to one in our church crypt, but as I said —" Anna's hand flapped so hard it looked like it might fly up into the choir loft with the stolen angels. "Yes?"

"Can we see the crypt?"

"Have your parents call to make a reservation." The guide handed Anna a brochure. "But we don't have tours this week; they're doing some restoration work down there. Now . . . if you'll turn to the left, you'll see our plaque in remembrance of Major John Pitcairn. . . ."

Anna frowned at the brochure.

"Pitcairn was fatally wounded while rallying the Royal Marines at the Battle of Bunker Hill," the guide continued. "He died on June 17, 1775. His body is interred beneath this church."

This time, Henry's hand shot up.

"Yes?"

"Is he in that crypt place?"

"Yes."

"So where is it?"

"Beneath the church."

"How do you get down there?"

"If you are on an official tour, you use the staircase up front. Otherwise" — the guide looked at Henry over her glasses — "you don't. Now, if you'll all come to the back of the church, I'll share a few more historical tidbits and then escort you to the gift shop."

Anna started to follow, but Henry grabbed her sleeve. "Hang on," he whispered, and ducked into one of the pews. He slid down to make room for Anna and José, and they stayed out of sight until everybody else left.

"Let's check that crypt *now*," Henry said.

Anna nodded. "She said the stairs were up here. Follow me." She started toward the front of the church, as if this whole thing were her idea. Henry doubted they'd find anything, but the tunnels sounded cool. His Storm the Castle video game had a labyrinth where you had to explore a maze of shrubbery and peek around dark corners. He was really good at it.

Anna opened the door at the front of the church. "Jackpot!" A set of twirly wooden stairs spiraled down into the dark.

José flipped a switch, and a naked lightbulb lit the stairs. They climbed down to a long hallway, all bricked in on the sides with rust-red pipes running along the ceiling. Henry had to duck to keep from bumping his head.

José coughed, and Henry felt his own throat tickle. The air felt musty and dusty and thick.

Anna unfolded her crumpled brochure. "This says the crypt contains thirty-seven tombs. With more than eleven hundred bodies."

"Whoa . . ." Henry felt the narrow hallways squeeze a little narrower. "So where are they all?"

"Here, I think." José ran his hand over a plaque embedded in the bricks on one wall. It read ANN RUGGLES TOMB 1742. Underneath was a small, bricked-in doorway.

"They're all over," Henry said, wandering down the hall. Some tombs were boarded up. Others had doors, as if you could knock and somebody might answer from the other side.

Anna walked along, reading names. "Samuel Watts and Peter Dickerman. This one just says 'Stranger's Tomb.' And here's — oh!"

Henry and José rushed over to see the tomb where Anna was standing. There was no name plaque above it, but whoever it was, they'd been disturbed. Someone had broken through the wooden door. Jagged pieces of splintered wood littered the floor.

"That damage looks new," Henry whispered.

Anna's eyes got huge. "Like it happened last night. Right after the painting was stolen!"

Henry couldn't stop staring into the dark. "Are you sure this is a tomb? It looks like it keeps going. What if it's the tunnel that —"

A clanging sound interrupted him, echoing off the bricks behind them. Henry's heart catapulted into his throat. "Someone's coming!"

"What if it's that tour guide?" Anna's face twisted with worry.

But the voices that drifted down the hall were deep and gruff.

"What if it's the Serpentine Princes?" José whispered.

"We gotta hide." Henry squatted down and tried to see into the dark opening past the arched doorway.

"We can't go in there," Anna whispered. "We don't even know —"

"We don't have a choice." Henry didn't want to squeeze into that dead-body darkness any more than Anna did, but there was nowhere else to hide. He ducked down, leaned deep into the opening, and crawled inside. Ahead of him, the blackness looked like it might go on forever. Behind him, the deep voices were getting louder.

Henry took one final look at the light, one last deep breath. "Follow me, you guys." And he scrambled into the dark.

FIVE

Spiderwebs tickled Henry's cheeks and trailed into his eyes as he crawled. Every so often, he felt José's hand brush against his ankle, and that made him feel better. At least he wasn't alone.

After a few minutes, Henry stopped, hoping to catch his breath, to let his heart settle down. But the darkness was so black, so heavy, it felt like it was pressing into his eyes, and that made his heart thump faster.

"You okay?" José whispered from behind him.

"Yeah," Henry answered. "Are you guys?"

"I hate this," Anna hissed. "Where does this even go? I think we should turn back."

"What if they're following us?" José's question hung in the air with the cobwebs.

Henry listened. Everything was quiet, but if they turned back, there was no telling who they'd meet in the dark. "This tunnel has to end somewhere, and once we get out the other end, we'll be able to get back to that pizza place." Henry was glad his voice sounded more confident than he felt. He was tired and worried about Dad and Bethany and the baby and hungry, too. At least there'd be food at the pizza place. "I say we keep going forward."

"If everyone is moving forward together, success takes care of itself," José whispered. "Henry Ford said that."

"This is so not what Henry Ford meant," Anna grouched. "Keep going. It smells in here."

Henry started crawling again, but he couldn't move fast. It was hard to know how far they'd gone when he finally stretched a hand out in front of him and felt something other than empty dark.

"I think we're at the end!" he whispered. "This is . . ." He slid his hand over the smooth stone in front of him until he found an edge. He traced it with his fingers. "It's one of those little doorways!"

"Thank goodness!" Anna whispered behind him. "Is it open?"

"Uh . . . no." And no matter how much Henry felt around, he couldn't find a handle or doorknob. He pushed the door with both hands, but it didn't budge.

"Hold on a second . . ." Henry wiggled around until his feet were facing the doorway. He leaned against José and kicked the door, but it didn't move. "You guys . . . I need you to push on me when I say go. As hard as you can, and don't let me slip, okay?"

"All right, hold on."

Henry felt José's bony hands on his shoulders.

"Is Anna backing you up?" Henry asked.

Her voice came from behind José. "Yes. Tell me when you're going to push."

"Ready . . ." Henry bent his legs and put both feet flat against the door.

"Set . . ." He stretched his arms out to the sides to brace himself against the tunnel walls.

He took a deep breath — *"Go!"* — and pushed as hard as he could to straighten his legs. José's fingers dug into Henry's shoulders, and the tunnel walls scratched his hands, but the door was finally starting to move. "Keep pushing!" he panted.

With one last grunt, he kicked again and felt something give way. The door swung open with a sharp groan, and Henry found his legs flailing into an open, dark space. He lowered himself out of the tunnel to the floor and blinked. A sliver of light spilled in from above the far wall, and Henry's eyes adjusted as José and Anna climbed down. "Look!" Henry whispered.

Big cardboard boxes were stacked along the walls of the room.

"Ohmygosh!" Anna squealed. "This must be where they brought the stolen art!"

"But there are so many of them," José said.

"I *know*! What if . . . what if the Serpentine Princes have been hiding stolen loot here for ages?" Anna rushed to one of the boxes and started picking at the packing tape that sealed the top. "You guys, this is *huge*! This could be — what if the Rembrandts and Vermeer from the original Isabella Stewart Gardner Museum heist are here?"

"Anna," José began, "we don't even know where we are. This might be —"

Before he could finish, the room filled with light so bright it made Henry's eyes water.

"I'll tell you where you are. On *private* property! And when the police arrive, you're — oh! It's you three!" Their tour guide stood in the doorway.

"Uh . . . sorry." Anna's voice was weak. She was kneeling by that big cardboard box, her hands tangled in the packing tape she'd finally managed to get loose. "We . . . it probably sounds crazy, but we found that tunnel and then we thought somebody was chasing us, so . . ."

"That *somebody* was our security staff. Whatever possessed you to break into the crypt?"

"We didn't technically break in," José said. "The door was unlocked. And someone had already pried those boards off the tunnel entrance."

"I told you there's restoration work happening in the crypt. That's why it's not open this week." The woman folded her arms. "But, of course, you weren't paying attention to that information."

"We couldn't really wait." Anna kept talking faster and faster. "When you mentioned the tunnel, we thought maybe the thieves who hit the Gardner museum last night had used it to hide stuff."

"Like that pirate you talked about." Henry hoped he'd get points for having paid attention. "With the angels?"

The woman was totally not impressed.

"And then we thought maybe these boxes were full of . . ." Anna stopped talking and looked down at her tape-tangled hands.

"Full of what?" the woman barked.

"Priceless stolen art," José said quietly, "but we're guessing now that's probably not the case."

"Well, let's see. . . ." The guide stepped up to the box closest to Anna and ripped off the last of the packing tape. She plunged her arm inside, pulled out a fuzzy green stuffed animal wearing a Boston Red Sox jersey, dangled it by one red sneaker, and raised her eyebrows. "Does this meet your criteria for priceless stolen art?"

A cell phone in the lady's pocket started playing a fife and drum song. She tossed the stuffed animal back in the box and answered. "Yeah? Good. I'll bring them right up." She put the phone away, looked at Anna, and pointed to a set of stairs on the other side of the room. "Get moving, Nancy Drew. All of you. The police are waiting upstairs."

SIX

"Here you go!" The tour guide delivered Henry, Anna, and José to the two Boston police officers waiting by the penny candy rack in the Old North Church gift shop.

"So these are the trespassers," one officer said, popping a fireball in his mouth.

The tour guide nodded. "Our security guys caught 'em down in the crypt. They took off through that tunnel we've got open for restoration. It leads right into the gift shop basement, so Tony waited in the crypt, and I came to head 'em off." The woman nodded with satisfaction. "They're all yours."

Henry wished they could explain themselves. But they couldn't exactly tell the truth about being junior members of a secret society to protect the world's artifacts. Even if they had, it would have sounded totally dumb. Secret societies had always seemed stupid and fake to Henry, too, until he ended up in one.

Finally, José shrugged and said, "We didn't make a very smart choice. We're sorry to have alarmed everyone."

One of the officers sighed. "Where are your parents?"

Anna looked at José.

José looked at Henry.

Henry looked out the window. The grown-ups were in their Silver Jaguar Society meeting at that dumpy pizza place, but he couldn't say that, either. That was the problem with secret societies. They were so secret all the time.

"They're having lunch," José said.

"Okay." The officer pulled out his phone and held it up. "How can I reach them?"

"Well . . ." José took a deep breath. "My mom's cell phone is 802 —"

"Here they come!" Anna pointed out the window, where people were suddenly hurrying down the street from the direction of the pizza place. Her mom and Aunt Lucinda were leading the pack, looking around frantically.

Henry tapped on the glass of the gift shop's front window and waved.

They waved for him to come outside, just as the

police officer stepped up next to Henry and motioned for the parents to come in.

"We are in so much trouble," Anna said as the grown-ups waited to cross the street.

Henry looked out the window and saw a steady stream of Silver Jaguar Society members hurrying down the street in clusters of twos and threes. Some headed for the subway. Some jumped into cabs, and a few piled into a waiting van. They all carried duffel bags or backpacks and had their hands full of papers.

"Isn't that Michael?" José pointed to a tall, dark-haired man getting into a cab. It was the society member who owned the lodge where Henry, Anna, and José had stayed in Costa Rica. José waved, but the cab sped away before Michael saw him.

"Look at 'em all. There's Snake-Arm!" Henry waved to another man hurrying down the street. Snake-Arm's real name was Claude Pickersgill, and he had helped to investigate the flag heist in Washington, DC.

"Where on earth did you go?" Anna's mother asked as she burst into the gift shop with José's parents and Henry's aunt behind her. Then she saw the police officers. "Is everything all right here?"

"Your children have been trespassing on private property, ma'am."

Henry, Anna, and José listened as the grown-ups fibbed their way through an explanation. José's mom told the cops about the "family reunion history tour of Boston" and explained that the kids were "mystery novel fans with vivid imaginations." Then Anna's mom happened to mention that her husband was a United States senator, and that seemed to convince the officers that they could release the kids with no charges being filed.

"Don't you ever do something like this again." Aunt Lucinda rushed Henry down the street. She stopped at a dark blue van with tinted windows and waited, looking up and down the street, even up at the rooftops, while José's dad unlocked the doors. Henry climbed into the back and slid over to make room for Aunt Lucinda and José. Anna and her mom claimed the middle seats, and José's parents sat in front.

Aunt Lucinda shook her head as the van started down the narrow street. She was looking out the window, squeezing a rolled-up bunch of papers in her hands. "Henry, you need to follow my directions from here on out. *All* of you. Things are escalating, and when we get to Paris —"

Henry, Anna, and José all spoke at the same time.

"What?"

"Where?"

"*Paris?!*"

"Yes, Paris." Aunt Lucinda unrolled her tube of

papers. They were boarding passes for a flight from Boston to Paris leaving at — Henry tipped his head to see the time — eight o'clock that night. José and Anna were already peppering their parents with questions.

"What about school?"

"You'll be missing a few days. It's already arranged."

"But we don't have clothes or anything."

"Yes, you do. We packed for you."

"We can't just leave!" Henry blurted. "What's going on with the baby? Have you even talked to Dad?"

Aunt Lucinda took a deep breath. "Yes. And he thinks it's best that you come with me. The baby was early but she's . . . stable."

Aunt Lucinda's voice didn't sound stable. And Henry knew from back at the gift shop that Aunt Lucinda was a pretty good liar. "What do you mean, stable? Tell me the truth."

She sighed. "The baby is in intensive care, having some trouble breathing on her own." She looked out the window and called up to the front. "Not this way! Take a left, and we'll get on the highway." She turned back to Henry. "Soon, we hope she'll be strong enough to go home, but for now, your dad and Bethany are going to stay with her. They're not leaving her side."

Aunt Lucinda said that as if she thought it would make Henry feel better. It should have; Henry knew that. But he couldn't help thinking, *What about me?*

"*Why* are we going to Paris?" Henry must have said it louder than he meant to because the whole van went quiet, and José looked back with a worried face. "I mean . . . I think we deserve to know what's going on," Henry said, trying to keep his voice even.

"You do," Aunt Lucinda said, peering out the window at the brick buildings rushing past. "We'll fill you in once we get you to the airport and you're safe."

Her last word hung in the air, and Henry thought about what she meant.

They'd be safe at the airport.

Until they got there, they weren't.

SEVEN

At the airport, Aunt Lucinda led everyone — no, *herded* them through security.

"Do you have any liquids, chemicals, sharp objects, or firearms in your bag?" the security lady asked Henry.

"Beats me." He glared at Aunt Lucinda. "I didn't pack it."

Aunt Lucinda swooped in — "No, no, of course not" — and the security people let Henry go through the body scanner and on to their gate. Henry had hoped they'd stop him, say, "No, this boy can't go to Paris! Not when he didn't even pack his own bag. He belongs here in Boston with his dad!"

"This is so amazing," Anna said as she took her laptop from her backpack and turned to Henry. "Did you know I speak French? *Bonjour! Où sont les toilettes?* That means *where's the bathroom.*"

"Leave me alone." Henry took out his SuperGame-Prism-5000, loaded Zombie-Robot Apocalypse, and started jabbing at the buttons. What was his dad thinking, letting Aunt Lucinda drag him to Paris? Lately, it felt like other people were in charge of his whole life.

Guess what, Henry? You're a junior member of the Silver Jaguar Society now!

Guess what, Henry? We're moving to Boston with Bethany!

Guess what, Henry? You're a big brother!

Guess what, Henry? You're going with Aunt Lucinda because we're too busy with the baby and need you out of the way.

"Careful," José said, leaning over to watch Henry play. "You're about to run into a zombie."

"I don't care," Henry said. The zombie jumped on him and sucked out his brains, and that was his last life, and it was time to get on the plane anyway.

The adults were still being all shushy and secretive, so José read his books, Anna scribbled in her notebook, and Henry started a new game. Eventually, he got so tired that even the weirdness of being whisked away to Europe couldn't keep him awake.

The next thing he knew, the plane landed with a bump.

"Ladies and gentlemen, welcome to Paris, where

the local time is seven thirty A.M. We hope you'll have a magical time in the City of Light."

It still felt like the middle of the night, and Henry was woozy with sleep. But José's mom and dad seemed wide awake as they hurried everyone off the plane, through the airport, down an escalator, and outside into the crisp morning air. "Go. Quickly! The blue van is ours."

The driver was an athletic-looking woman with snarly blond curls and pale skin that reddened at her cheeks. She barely acknowledged them when they approached, except to nod to Anna's mom. She pressed a button, the van's side door slid open, and they all climbed in.

It wasn't until they were all speeding away from the airport that Anna's mom and José's parents seemed to let out the breaths they'd been holding since the plane landed. Still, Aunt Lucinda kept turning around, peering out the rear window.

"If you're so worried about safety, why don't we call the police?" Henry whispered.

"Too risky. The society has been working with Interpol, which is an international group of investigators, but other than that —" She turned quickly and looked back again.

"Do we have shadows?" The woman driving looked in the mirror. She spoke with a British accent like the investigators in Henry's Tower of London game.

"No." Aunt Lucinda turned back to face front. "I think we're clear."

"Clear of *what*? Who are you looking for, and where are we going?" Anna blurted. Henry was glad she asked. His own head was so full of questions it felt like it might bust right open. "And who's *that*?" Anna looked at her mom and pointed toward the driver's seat in front of her.

Anna's mom sighed. "Anna, I want you to meet Miranda Blake. She manages a bookstore here in Paris. Miranda, this is my inquisitive daughter."

Miranda nodded in the mirror, but Anna ignored her. "Mom, what's going *on*?" Anna opened her notebook to the map she'd made in Boston. She leaned forward. "Do you *know* the Serpentine Prince gang did all this?"

"They've claimed responsibility for the thefts, with help from some other organized crime groups," her mom said. "And Goosen is demanding that his son be released from prison, or this will be just the beginning."

Anna scribbled like crazy, adding it all to her chart.

"It's like when Maldisio's partner gets taken into custody in Shadow Rogue Assassin," Henry said. "Maldisio kidnaps the queen's hairdresser and holds her for ransom to get his partner back."

"This is no game, Henry," Aunt Lucinda said. "The situation is escalating. These people have leveled a direct threat against members of the Silver Jaguar Society."

José's eyes got all big. "What did they say?"

"It's not what they said; it's what they've *taken* and the message it sends," Anna's mom said. "What you need to understand is that our group may be targeted. That includes me ... and Lucinda ... and José's mom. It includes all of you, too." She met each kid's eyes and let that sink in. "We also think a museum in Paris may still be at risk."

Anna started writing again. "So you guys are supposed to investigate that?"

"We're supposed to keep it from happening. If we can." José's mom sighed, like she didn't quite believe that was possible. His dad put an arm around her shoulder.

Anna bit her lip. "So how are you going to —"

But before she could finish, her mom said something in French to Miranda, and Miranda said something back, and Henry's aunt joined in, and pretty soon all the grown-ups were jabbering away in French.

"What are they saying?" Henry hissed.

Anna shrugged. "I can't tell. It's too fast and smooshed together."

Henry folded his arms and watched the traffic go by while words he didn't understand zipped around his head. After a while, the highway gave way to clogged city streets that got narrower and narrower until Miranda pulled up to a sidewalk crowded with pedestrians.

"Here we are." She pressed a button, and Henry's door slid open.

He grabbed his backpack, climbed down from the van, and stared at the store. It was painted green with lots of windows, and full of bookshelves that seemed to have spilled out the door onto the sidewalk. A yellow-and-black sign over the door read SHAKESPEARE AND COMPANY.

"That's not French." Anna sounded disappointed.

"It's an English bookstore," José's dad said, passing out luggage from the back of the van.

Henry looked at his duffel bag, then up at Aunt Lucinda. "Are we *staying* here?"

"You are. The adults have to go out soon and . . . may be a little while." She handed Henry an index card.

"In the rush to leave, I never set up my phone for international calling, so I want you to have this. In case of an emergency."

Henry looked down at the card. "Did you give Dad this number, too?"

"Yes, and I'm sure he'll call when he can." She led the kids through the store's wide-open green doors.

Anna's mother nodded to a young woman with short black hair who was working at a computer behind the counter. Then she headed for the back of the store, past tables with teetering stacks of books and a sculpture of some grumpy-looking guy staring out at the stacks.

"Dude looks like he's in charge of security." Henry patted the sculpture on the head.

"That dude," Aunt Lucinda said with a huff, "is William Shakespeare, the greatest playwright of all time and one of Miranda's ancestors. Now, the adults need to meet. You can take your bags up." She pointed toward some steps at the back of the store.

Henry, Anna, and José lugged their backpacks and duffel bags up the stairs while jazzy piano music drifted down.

"Oh, wow!" José pulled *Harry Potter and the Philosopher's Stone* from a bookshelf at the top. "This is a British edition first printing!" He plopped down on a bench and started reading.

Anna rolled her eyes. "Well, we won't see *him* for the rest of the trip." José loved Harry Potter even more than Henry loved video games.

Henry yawned. "Where do we go?" It wasn't even noon yet, but he was wiped out. He and Anna started down a hallway, where the music was louder.

The room at the end of the hall had walls covered in hand-drawn maps. A chess game was set up in one corner, and opposite that, a skinny blond teenager sat at the piano. He wore a black T-shirt and fedora, and his whole body swayed as his fingers flew up and down the keyboard. The song reminded Henry of the old big band music his mom used to love.

When it ended, Anna cleared her throat. "Um . . . *bonjour*?"

"Aren't you going to applaud?" the kid said with that same Tower of London accent. He spun around to face them and raised his eyebrows, waiting.

"Oh! Uh . . . sure." Anna clapped a few times. "You're really good."

"I know, right?" The kid looked at Henry, as if he wanted him to clap, too.

Henry didn't. "Hey, are there, like, places to sleep here?"

"There are!" The kid grinned and gestured toward a bench by the chessboard.

"Here?" Henry plopped down on the bench. It was like a rock. "You can't be serious."

The kid turned to Anna. "This one's a little wimpy for a member of such an elite group, isn't he?"

Anna gasped. "Oh! You're with the Silver Jaguar Society!"

"Oh, no." The kid shook his head and stepped toward them. "I'm a member of the Serpentine Princes."

Anna's mouth fell open, and she seemed frozen to the floorboards, but Henry sprang from the bench-bed, grabbed Anna's arm, and ran for the door. He forgot about that dumb chessboard, though, and tripped over the table, sending knights and pawns flying everywhere.

The piano kid laughed. "Relax. I'm Miranda's son — obviously not with the Serpentine Princes. I was having a bit of a joke on you." He grinned at Anna, who blushed and smiled back at him.

The kid held his hand out to Henry. "My name is Hem. No hard feelings?"

Henry got to his feet on his own. "What kind of name is that?"

"Only one I've got," Hem answered, swooping down to collect chess pieces from the floor. "Mum named me after the author Ernest Hemingway."

"Is your real name Hemingway?" Anna asked.

"Yeah. But I like Hem better." He shrugged. "Mostly I'm glad she didn't go with Ernest."

Anna laughed. Way too loud for a joke that wasn't even funny, Henry thought.

"Mum said there were three of you," Hem said. "Did you lose someone?"

"Oh! No . . . José's reading in here." They headed back to the other room, and Anna made introductions.

"Good to meet you." Hem nodded toward José's book. "Always happy to know a man who appreciates quality literature." He turned to Anna and Henry. "So it looks like we'll be spending some time together."

"Great." Henry crossed his arms. "Just great." He plopped down on a bigger bench with a thicker cushion and a velvet curtain pulled back on each side. The walls around it were covered in notes and pictures. "What is this, some kind of bulletin board?"

"Is there a note?" Hem rushed to the bench, and his eyes flew over the notes and drawings tacked everywhere.

"Yeah. About a million."

"Oh." Hem sounded disappointed. "Nothing new?"

"Who knows?" Henry stared at the cluttered wall. It looked as if people from all over the world had been here, and every one had left a note on some tiny scrap of paper. Some talked about how happy they were to be in Paris. Some left quotes from Shakespeare and Mark Twain and other people whose names José would probably recognize. The notes were held up with everything from tape to bobby pins to Band-Aids. One even looked like it might be stuck to the wall with — "Aw, man!" Henry rubbed his hand against the wall, trying to get the gum off his fingers.

Hem laughed. "Not everyone thinks to bring Scotch Tape."

Henry sniffed his hand. It smelled like spearmint. "Why'd you get all excited before?"

"I thought you'd spotted a society missive."

"A what?"

"A society missive. An official message." Hem looked at the three of them and tipped his head. "This bulletin board isn't really for tourists." He flicked at a couple notes with his hand. "It started that way, but then Mum realized it was the perfect place for society members to leave messages for one another."

"In a public bookstore?" Anna asked.

"Your parents told you this is the society's official safe house in Paris, didn't they?" Hem gestured toward the uncomfortable benches. "People sleep here all the time. It's always been known as a place for wandering writers. And since a bunch of them are descendants of *other* writers and artists . . .'"

"It became a sanctuary for the Silver Jaguar Society, too!" Anna finished. "That's why they brought us here." She bit her lip and looked up at the ceiling for a second, then back at Hem. "So do you know what our parents are up to?"

"Yeah. Trying to save what's left of the Louvre."

"Hem!" a voice called from downstairs.

"What?" he hollered back.

"Bring everyone down. We need to talk."

Hem sighed and stood up. "Mum's about to lay down the rules," he said, gesturing for them all to head downstairs. "And when she's finished," he whispered, grinning, "I'll tell you how we're going to break them."

EIGHT

"This is the best crepe on the Left Bank," Hem said, handing Henry a hot, folded-up pancake wrapped in thin paper.

"Yeah . . . thanks." Henry wouldn't have taken it except that he was starving. He couldn't stand Hem's dumb accent, especially since Anna seemed to like it enough for all of them. She'd totally given up on French and was starting to talk like Hem.

"Fon-tah-stick!" she said when she bit into her crepe.

Henry rolled his eyes, but after he took a bite of his, he had to admit it was actually pretty good. "What's in this?"

"Nutella and banana," Hem said, paying the street vendor. He unwrapped his own crepe and headed down the sidewalk along the river, away from Shakespeare and Company.

"Uh . . . guys?" José was lingering by the crepe stand. "Our parents said to get food and go right back to the bookstore."

It was true. As soon as the kids had come down those bookstore stairs, the grown-ups had surrounded them, and Hem's mom had gone over the rules. No sneaking out. No spying. And no discussion of the situation with *anyone*. Particularly with the concerns about someone leaking information to the Serpentine Princes. The adults were heading out to take care of "society business." The kids were staying at the store with Ursa, a society member who worked there, even though the only "work" Henry had seen her do so far was whisper into her cell phone and make kissy noises.

Hem's mom had given them money for food. "But come right back. Ursa will be here until the store closes at eleven. She'll call for Paul and Serge if there's any sign of trouble."

"They're like society bodyguards," Hem had whispered.

His mom had nodded. "I've asked Ursa to have them check on you from time to time anyway. No matter what, I want you to stay put."

"Even if we're not back," José's dad had added. "We

may be late, but we'll have keys, and under NO circumstances are you to open the door for anyone. Got it?"

José had nodded, answering for them all. "We understand."

Now José looked as if he might be stuck to the sidewalk with some of that gum from the bookstore bulletin board. "We can't just wander off. I mean . . . if you want to take a walk, we should at least call to see if it's okay, shouldn't we?"

Henry pulled Aunt Lucinda's index card from his pocket. He didn't think this counted as an emergency.

"What's that?" Hem was back at Henry's side in a second.

"Your mom's number, I guess," Henry said. "My aunt gave it to me in case we had issues."

"Well, we don't." Hem looked down at the card with the loopy C. "Your aunt has some seriously fancy handwriting." He sighed and took off his jacket. "Look, my friends . . . if we did what they said, we could be locked up for days." He looked up and down the river, then sidled up to José and gave him a good nudge with his shoulder. "Don't you want to see some of Paris while you're here?"

"I do," Anna said, wiping Nutella from her chin. "Is the Eiffel Tower nearby?"

"It's up the river a bit," Hem said, pointing. "Did

you know that it sparkles at night? Every hour on the hour, twenty thousand lightbulbs go off. It's spectacular."

Anna's eyes sparkled, too, when she heard that. "I'm not ready to go back to the store."

"Me neither," Henry said. Even hanging out with Hem and his stupid accent seemed like a better option than going back to those uncomfortable benches.

"Splendid," Hem said. "Then come with me." He started walking again, then turned to José and held out a wallet. "By the way, does this belong to you?"

José's eyes went all big, and his hand flew to his back pocket. "Yeah! How'd you get it? Did I drop it or something?"

"You're an easy target for pickpockets, my friend." Hem laughed, handing the wallet back. "Want to see how it's done?"

"I do!" Anna's face lit up.

Hem held up three fingers. "Three easy steps. First, misdirection." He turned to José. "Remember when I pointed to the river and nudged you? I was directing your attention away from me and creating a distraction." He bumped José again and, at the same time, reached for his wallet in slow motion. "The big action conceals the small one."

"That's brilliant," Anna said in her fake British accent.

Henry thought it was kind of jerky.

"Step two is concealment." Hem folded his jacket over his arm the way he'd had it back at the crepe stand. "This hides my hand — and your wallet after I've stolen it. And then step three is the getaway. I move on casually after I've made the lift, and you never notice what happened."

"Impressive," José said.

"Wow," Anna said, hurrying up to walk alongside Hem. "You're like a magician!"

"More like a criminal," Henry muttered. "So where are we going?"

"I'll show you." Hem pulled a paper from his pocket and unfolded it. It looked like one of the maps from the bookstore wall.

"Hmph," Henry said. "Did you steal that, too?"

"Steal it? I made it." Hem held the map so they could all see. "I kind of have a thing for maps."

"Nice," José said.

"That's beautiful," Anna gushed. "Do you copy them off the Internet or what?"

Hem scoffed. "These are *my* maps. Drawn from the rooftop of Notre-Dame, mostly. You can see all of Paris from up there." He pointed to a drawing of the cathedral, then traced the streets leading to a palace-like building near the river. "This is where we're going now. Musée du Louvre."

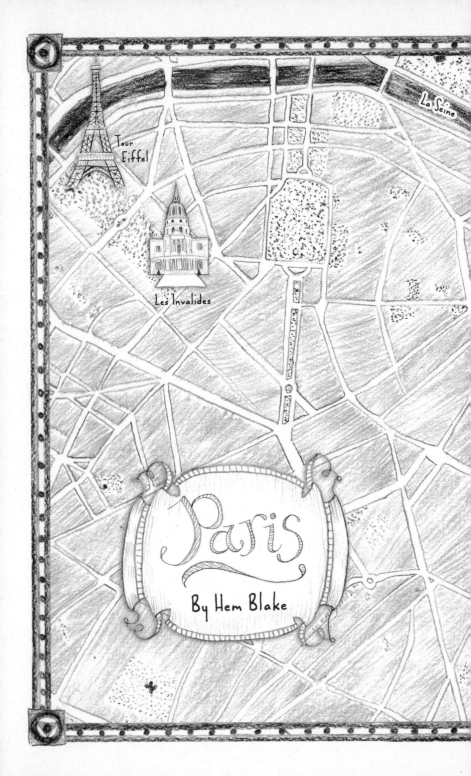

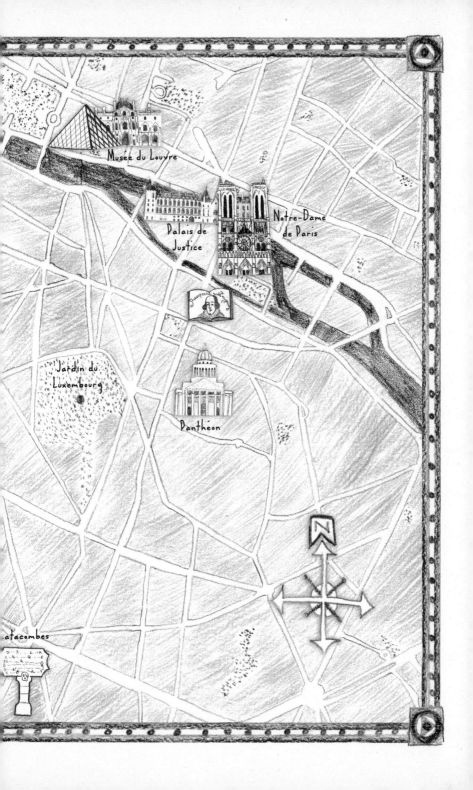

He folded up the map, tucked it away, and led them toward a bridge. They wandered along the row of riverside souvenir stands that sold tiny Eiffel Towers and reproductions of the *Mona Lisa* in every size imaginable.

"So, Hem . . . the Louvre is the museum our parents think may still be at risk?" Anna was half running to keep up with him. "From what we heard, the society thinks Goosen is doing all this for his son. Like if he has enough art, he'll be able to trade it for his son's freedom."

"Enough art . . . and perhaps some of the people in charge of protecting it." Hem turned onto the bridge.

"Wait, what?" Henry squeezed in between Hem and Anna. "What people does he have?"

"None yet." Hem stepped up to the railing and looked up the river toward the big cathedral. "But with the last museums to be hit — the American targets — there was a clear pattern to what was taken."

"We heard there was some kind of threat, but I don't really get it." Anna frowned. "They stole a Van Gogh from the National Gallery in Washington, and then the Isabella Stewart Gardner portrait from Boston."

"They got a Degas self-portrait from the Met . . . and a Frida Kahlo self-portrait from the Albright-

Knox Gallery in Buffalo," José said slowly, and then, "Oh! Those are all . . ."

"Society members. Frida Kahlo was your ancestor, wasn't she?" Hem asked José, who nodded. "So I'm guessing you three heard about the two failed heists as well as the ones that succeeded?"

Henry shook his head.

"One was at the Revere House," Hem said, looking right at Anna. "The other was at the Smithsonian Museum of American History, where —"

"Are you serious?" Henry interrupted. Even before Hem finished, Henry knew he had to be talking about the original Star-Spangled Banner. "They didn't get the flag, did they?"

"Not this time." Hem started walking again, and the others followed. "But we know they're planning more, and Mum agrees those last heists were meant to send a message."

"A message to who?" Henry said.

"Whom," Hem said.

"Whatever." Henry wanted to shove this guy, but he wanted information more. "A message to whom?"

"Us." Hem turned off the bridge and jogged across the street.

Henry, Anna, and José rushed to catch up before the light changed.

"Us?" Anna said. "Us, meaning society members?"

Hem nodded, hurrying down the sidewalk. It ran alongside a garden and a mansion that took up the whole block. "Think about it," he said, turning left. "What message does it send when somebody targets specific pieces of art created by the ancestors of society members? When they go after those particular paintings, one by one?"

"Oh . . ." Henry felt a chill that he was pretty sure had nothing to do with the Paris wind. "I think I get it."

Hem nodded. "The message comes through loud and clear, don't you think? Watch out. And back off. Or you'll be next."

NINE

"Students don't have to pay, so we can use this entrance." Hem waved Anna, José, and Henry through a gate into the Louvre's big, open lobby and pointed up a wide set of stairs. "We'll start in the Denon wing."

"Start what?" Henry hoped this wasn't going to be like one of Aunt Lucinda's marathon museum visits.

"My personal tour of the Louvre. I want to see for myself what's missing. Mum and the other society members talked about a Vermeer and a Monet, but the museum said there were smaller pieces stolen, too."

They all followed Hem up the stairs, but only Anna looked excited about the tour.

"Here's stop number one," Hem said, gazing up at a headless marble statue with wings. "*Winged Victory.*"

"Wow," Anna said.

"Does the museum know her head got stolen?" Henry asked.

"Henry!" Anna gave him a look.

Hem laughed. "The sculpture was like this when it was discovered on a Greek island. It's been here since 1884. Except for a few years during World War Two . . ." He lowered his voice. "Society members moved *Victory* and a bunch of other pieces out of Paris to keep them safe from the bombs." He pointed up another set of stairs to the right. "Come on, let's go see the *Mona Lisa* before the room gets too busy."

Hem took the next set of stairs two at a time, led them through a hallway of old Italian paintings he called *frescoes*, and stepped into a long gallery full of paintings and sculptures. There was one of a mom with an infant, and it reminded Henry of his new baby sister. When would his dad call? He was probably still really busy with the baby. But didn't he wonder how Henry was doing in Paris, way across the ocean? Henry looked away from the painting and hurried to catch up with the others.

"Is the *Mona Lisa* up there?" Anna pointed to a group of people ahead.

"No," Hem said, squinting. "It's . . . oh." His voice fell. "It *was* a painting called *Old Man with a Young Boy*."

He led Henry, Anna, and José through the crowd to an empty spot on the wall.

"Was it a well-known painting?" José asked.

Hem shook his head. "That's the weird thing. It's not super-famous like the *Mona Lisa* or anything, but I fancied it." He blinked fast, and Henry felt a little bad for Hem, even though he still hated his accent and that he used words like *fancied*.

"Let's keep going. She's in here." Hem directed them into a big room with one area roped off. Behind the ropes, a thick wooden semicircle of railing — almost like a counter where you'd order ice cream — surrounded an empty glass box.

"Umm . . ." Henry had heard people say the *Mona Lisa* was smaller than you'd think, but he couldn't see anything in that case. He turned to Hem. "Dude . . . where is she?"

Hem's face filled with alarm for a second. Then he hurried over to the guard at the edge of the railing. They talked, and the guard gestured toward the empty glass case, then off to the side.

"Well?" Anna asked when Hem returned.

"Everything's okay," Hem said. "They've taken her for some restoration work."

Henry frowned. "They move the *Mona Lisa* around like that? Isn't it a security risk?"

"I know, right?" Anna agreed. "Like the Jaguar Cup . . ." The golden cup had been stolen in Costa Rica, on its way to an international exhibit.

"And that painting in the book *Chasing Vermeer*,"

José added. "The girl writing the letter? Wasn't that out on loan when it was stolen?"

Henry nodded. "Same thing happens in my Super-Heist game when the museum sends the *Starry Night* painting to get re-starred."

"There's a video game where *Starry Night* gets stolen?" Anna asked.

"Totally," Henry said. "There are like a dozen paintings to steal. If you win, you go back to your sim house at the end and decide where to hang 'em all."

"But that's fiction, and so is the Vermeer thing, actually." José looked at Hem. "When the *Mona Lisa* is being restored, do they do that here at the museum?"

"They do," Hem said. But he frowned at the empty glass case.

Anna sighed. "Well, that stinks. I was going to write about seeing the *Mona Lisa* for my school paper."

"If the painting's on vacation, I guess you'll have to take a break, too," Henry said.

Anna looked offended. "News doesn't go on vacation." She turned to Hem. "What else should we see?"

"The Egyptian wing. It's spectacular." Hem led them through the maze of the museum to a big hall crowded with statues of Egyptian gods and slabs of stone filled with hieroglyphics. "And look at this." He led them to a smaller, darker room and pointed to a tattered, wrapped-up something on a shelf in a glass case. "It's a cat mummy."

"No way!" Anna stepped closer to read the information card. "I had no idea cats had mummies."

"All cats have mummies," Henry said. "Daddies, too."

Anna rolled her eyes, but Hem laughed as they headed for the European art halls. He seemed relieved to find a Vermeer painting. "Thank God," he said. "*The Astronomer* is safe."

But *The Lacemaker* was gone. And not far from that empty spot on the wall, two more paintings had been stolen. One was a snowy landscape by Claude Monet. The other was by a painter named Camille Corot. "It was a sailboat," Hem said. "A really spectacular one. The sky behind it was all moody." He looked at the empty places on the wall and lowered his voice. "I have this weird feeling that Vincent Goosen and I have the same taste in art."

José nodded slowly. "Like Harry Potter and Voldemort. They're on opposite sides, but there's this weird connection, and in some ways they have a lot in common."

"Goosen was a society member once," Anna said thoughtfully. "You really think he's stealing his favorite stuff?"

"I do," Hem said. He took a deep breath. "And I have an even worse feeling that he's not quite finished."

"Why do you say that?" José asked.

Before Hem could answer, an alarm sounded,

whooping through the gallery. It was so loud Henry thought it might shatter the glass cases.

"*Attention, s'il vous plaît . . .*"

"What?" Anna shouted over the blaring alarms.

As if he'd heard her, the man on the loudspeaker repeated his message in English: "Attention please, visitors. Due to a security breach, we must evacuate the museum. Please proceed to the nearest exit immediately."

TEN

"It's probably nothing," Hem said as they rushed out of the museum, but his voice sounded shaky.

They crossed the street and headed toward the bridge that would take them across the Seine and back to the bookstore. Below, a boxy-looking boat was pulling away from the riverbank. "What's that?" José asked. "I've seen a few of them today."

"Batobus," Hem said, veering down a staircase along the sidewalk. "Come down and have a look. They're like water taxis."

Hem led them down to a booth by the water where a sign displayed the boat's route, from the Louvre to another stop called Champs-Élysées, then to the Eiffel Tower.

"It goes up to Notre-Dame, too," José said. "Near the bookstore, right?"

"Indeed," Hem said. "Fancy a ride?"

"I fancy dinner," Henry said. "That crepe was good, but I'm starving again."

"I think we can take care of that." Hem led them back up the steps and over the bridge to an open storefront. The painted sign outside called it a *boulangerie*.

Hem ordered them some food, and Henry was ogling the baguettes under the glass when a scrawny teenager came racing down the sidewalk. A black handbag flew behind him like a wild kite as he knocked Henry into the deli counter, splashed through a fountain with dragons spitting water, and crossed the street.

"Dude! Did you see that guy take off?" Henry said. "He was —"

"Watch out!" Hem grabbed Anna's elbow and pulled her out of the way as a security guard dressed in black pants and a crisp white shirt came tearing out of a store. He chased after the kid, pumping his arms, and was starting to catch up when the teenager leaped over a fence and disappeared down some stairs below a yellow sign that read: METROPOLITAIN.

The guard followed, but Hem shook his head. "He'll never get him down there."

Sure enough, the security guy came back in less than a minute, purse-less and wiping sweat from his forehead.

"Pickpockets and purse snatchers know this area's crawling with tourists. You have to be aware." Hem

looked at José. "That's why I took your wallet earlier —
not just to have a joke on you. Paris is a dream come
true for thieves."

"Looks like that one got away," José said.

"*Voilà,*" the bald guy at the counter said, holding
out four baguettes wrapped in paper.

"Lots of them get away," Hem said, paying for the
food. "That bloke ran down to the Métro, probably
jumped the tracks, and vanished into the tunnels. It's
easy to disappear down there. This Paris that you see
in the sunlight" — he gestured down the street toward
Notre-Dame — "is mirrored underground. The whole
city is riddled with tunnels, left over from the lime-
stone quarries hundreds of years ago."

"Under us now?" Henry stomped his foot on the
sidewalk. It sounded pretty solid.

"All over." Hem took a bite of his sandwich, and
gooey cheese oozed out the side.

"Does anybody use them anymore?" Anna asked.

Hem swallowed. "Not officially," he said, "but
cataphiles have discovered a million ways to make
them useful again."

"What's a cater-feel?" Henry asked.

"Cah-ta-feeeyls" — Hem drew the word out — "are
people who go down into the tunnels whenever they
can find access, through a loosened manhole cover or
passage in an underground garage."

"Go down and do what?" Anna asked.

"Explore. There are underground cemeteries, rock formations from the water dripping. And many cataphiles are members of the UX."

"UX?" José asked.

"Urban eXperiment. It's a clandestine group that uses the underground tunnel network to get access to all sorts of sites and government buildings. They try to expose flaws in museum security. Sometimes, they hold film festivals underground. And they restore the history down there." Hem's whole face came alive as he described it. "One tunnel was a Nazi bunker during World War Two."

"They just let people run around down there?" Henry thought it sounded like too much fun to be allowed.

"Ah, no," Hem answered. "The city of Paris has declared the tunnels officially off-limits."

"People go down *illegally*?" José looked worried, but Anna's eyes lit up, and Henry could tell she was writing another newspaper story in her head.

"It is technically illegal," Hem said, "but we do no harm. In fact —"

"Wait, *we*?" Henry's jaw dropped. "We, as in you're one of them? You've been there?"

Hem raised his eyebrows and shrugged. "Perhaps a time or two. I've made some splendid maps of the place." He polished off the last of his sandwich and stepped into the river of people crossing the square.

"Do you see other people down there?" Henry asked, catching up to Hem as they headed back toward the bookstore.

"No. That's the beauty of it." Hem sighed as they waited to cross the street. A car horn blared at a pedestrian who ventured out too soon. "And so quiet. No taxis or buses or sirens. Only the dripping of water and your own breath in your ears. On the rare occasion that you do run into someone, they're always friendly. Cataphiles . . ." He paused at the door to the bookstore. "We take care of one another. It's like a family, almost like —"

"The Silver Jaguar Society?" José said softly.

"Almost," Hem said, pulling open the door. "Yes, almost."

But before any of them could step inside, another man came flying down the street — no bag in his hand, no stolen wallet — but his face looked just as intense as he raced up to them. He grabbed Hem's elbow, blurted something in French, and then took off again, racing down the street toward Notre-Dame. But not before Henry noticed the jaguar pendant hanging at his throat.

Whatever he said, his words nearly brought Hem to his knees. He grabbed the door frame for support.

"What is it?" Anna asked. "What's going on?"

"They did it," Hem said. "They got the *Mona Lisa*."

ELEVEN

The jaguar-pendant man was gone before the kids could ask a single question, so they headed into the bookstore. Ursa was behind the counter with her phone pressed to her ear. "Hold on one second, love," she cooed, then raised her eyebrows at Hem's frantic face. "What's happening?"

"Did you hear?" Anna began. "They —"

"Evacuated the Louvre!" Hem shouted, loud enough to drown out whatever Anna was going to say next. "Probably related to the investigation." Ursa nodded and went back to her cell-phone boyfriend.

Anna turned to Hem. "What about —"

Henry kicked her shoe, low enough so the counter blocked Ursa's view but hard enough to shut Anna up. "Let's go upstairs. I'm beat."

"I need to use the restroom," Hem said. "I'll be up in a bit."

Anna scowled, but she followed Henry and José up the worn wooden staircase and flopped down on the cushiony bench under the bulletin board. "Why'd you kick me? Ursa's in charge tonight. Don't you think she should know what's going on?"

Henry shook his head. "Hem didn't want to tell her."

Anna made a face. "Since when do you care what Hem thinks?"

"I just —" Henry couldn't answer that. Hem's accent and fancy British words still bugged him, but anybody who explored off-limits underground tunnels in the dark couldn't be totally uncool. "I think we should hear what he has to say."

"Was this open before?" José asked. He was standing by a window that led out to a second-story courtyard. It was surrounded by walls on four sides, and somebody had set up a bunch of plants with little gnomes peeking out of them.

Henry shrugged. "I dunno. Maybe a gnome got bored and came in to get something to read."

José closed the window, came back to the cushiony bench, sprawled out, and started reading the little notes on the wall.

Anna sighed. "Anything new?"

"One from a kid in Texas," José said, studying a

tiny scrap of paper. "She drew a picture of herself and says she has three dogs."

"That was there before." Anna crawled over José's knees to look at the jumble of papers. "But I don't think this one was." She knelt on the cushion and squinted up at a scribbled-on orange square. "Somebody squeezed a whole John Milton poem onto this napkin."

Henry leaned over to see. His English teacher, Mr. Sharp, loved reading aloud and shared poems once in a while. Some of those were cool, but this one didn't make any sense.

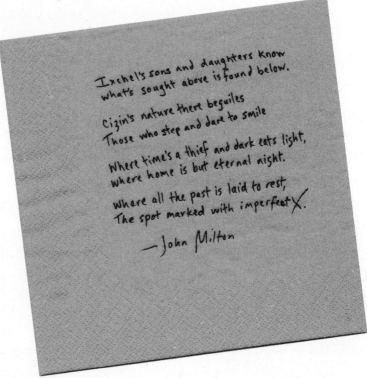

Ixchel's sons and daughters know
what's sought above is found below.

Cizin's nature there beguiles
Those who step and dare to smile

Where time's a thief and dark eats light,
where home is but eternal night.

Where all the past is laid to rest,
The spot marked with imperfect X.

— John Milton

"That John Milton guy must have been out there," Henry said, nudging José aside and stretching out on the bench.

"Are you kids hungry or anything?" Ursa asked as she stepped into the reading nook.

"No thanks," Anna said.

"I hope you haven't been getting into trouble." Ursa smiled and sat down on the edge of Henry's bench. Her eyes scanned the wall of paper scraps and settled on the poem.

"That one's new, isn't it?" Anna said. "Somebody's a Milton fan."

Ursa didn't answer right away. She must have been a Milton fan, too, because she looked at the poem a long time before she said, "It's interesting what people choose to share, isn't it? Well . . ." She stood up and started back downstairs. "Let me know if you need anything."

"Hem's been gone awhile," José whispered after Ursa left. "Do you think he took off to find that guy?"

"I dunno. He's probably down in some tunnel, or up on a roof drawing another map." Henry couldn't quite figure Hem out. "Let's check downstairs."

On their way down, they passed Ursa, carrying a pile of limp-looking pillows. "Thought you might sleep better with an extra pillow or two," she said. "I'll leave them for you."

"Thanks," Anna said, and they squeezed against the staircase wall so she could pass.

Hem was just coming inside when they got to the front of the store.

"Where'd you go?" Henry asked.

"Out to make a call." He pulled a cell phone from his pocket and looked down at it, frowning. "Wanted to make sure Mum knows about what happened, but she didn't pick up."

He peered past them, into the shadows at the back of the store, then whispered, "Where's Ursa?"

"Upstairs," Anna said. "How come?"

"I don't fancy her knowing all our business." He pulled Henry, Anna, and José behind a high bookshelf and lowered his voice. "This situation with the *Mona Lisa* is . . . Well, you've heard the society is concerned someone may be sharing information with Goosen, yes?"

Anna nodded. "Like a double agent, right?"

"Exactly," Hem whispered, "and I'm not pointing fingers at Ursa, but I do think —"

"Seriously?" Henry almost laughed. "You think the grown-ups would leave us with Ursa if there was a chance she's the one who —"

"Shh!" Hem glared at Henry. "I think the fewer people who know about this latest development, the better."

"We have to tell our parents at least," José said. "My mom's not going to believe this. After everything —"

"Not going to believe what?" Ursa asked, stepping out from the other side of the bookshelf.

"That I . . . managed to order my own food. In French." José smiled.

"He did great," Anna added. "I helped him translate."

Henry rolled his eyes. Even in a pointless made-up story, she had to be a know-it-all.

"Well, isn't that something!" Ursa gave José a pat on the shoulder, then hurried behind him to get her jacket from the coat tree near the door. Her cell phone chimed with a text message, and she looked down with a goofy smile. Then she turned back to the kids. "I'm sure your mums and all will be along before it gets too late. I'm going to close up shop a bit early and go meet a friend. Unless you'd like me to wait a bit?"

Hem shook his head. "No, I'm sure they'll be back soon."

"Good, then. I'll have Serge and Paul keep an eye on the place overnight. Gilbert will open in the morning, and then I'll be along by eleven or so. Hem has my number if you need anything before then." She waved her phone at them as she left, locking the door behind her.

"Who's Gilbert?" Anna asked.

"Older chap who works here sometimes. He lives in an apartment on the block." Hem went to the window and peered through the shutters. "I wonder how much Ursa knows about the Louvre. Have you been upstairs to see if there are any messages?"

"We were up there," Henry said. "The only thing new was some weird poem."

"What did it say?"

Anna wrinkled her nose. "I don't think it even had a title. It was kind of like a riddle. Ixchel's sons and daughters know what's found below . . . or above . . . or something like that."

Hem's eyes widened. "That's not a poem. It's a message!" And he raced for the back of the store.

TWELVE

By the time Henry, Anna, and José got up the stairs, Hem was standing in the middle of a swirling, paper-scrap mess. The window was wide open again, and the wind had freed a whole bunch of papers from their thumbtacks and Band-Aids.

Hem stood in front of the wall. "Where is it?"

"It's . . . it was right here." Henry pointed. "But it's gone." He kicked at the notes scattered on the wooden floor, but they were all written on scraps of paper. There wasn't an orange napkin to be found.

"Was Ursa up here?" Hem's eyes narrowed.

"She brought up pillows and stuff, but I doubt she would have taken the note." Anna shook her head. "She saw it before and didn't act like it was any big deal. I don't think she even knew it was a message."

"Who says it was?" Henry scoffed. "It didn't even make sense."

"It was. It must have been." Hem paced back and forth.

Anna walked over to the window, pushed it shut, and turned the latches to lock it. "Did you lock this when you closed it before?" she asked José.

"I don't think so. I'm not sure."

Hem let out a frustrated sigh. "Someone must have come in while we were downstairs."

"Who would want to steal a poem off the wall?" José asked.

"Someone who wants to intercept a Silver Jaguar Society message." Hem looked out the window. "Someone with access to one of these apartments with windows on the courtyard."

"Is that the only way onto this little roof?" Anna looked out the window.

Hem nodded. "Gilbert lives over there." He pointed across to an apartment with spider plants hanging in the window. "We go through his apartment sometimes if the storefront is being watched and we don't want to be seen."

"Maybe *he* stole the note," José said. "They think someone's slipping information to the Serpentine Princes, right? What if —"

"No." Hem shook his head. "Gilbert has been with

the store — and the society — more then twenty years. There's no way he'd do that."

"That's what I thought about my captain of the guards in Storm the Castle," Henry said. "And then he totally turned on me. You never know."

"Well, *I* know." Hem frowned. "Someone else must have come across from a different apartment to nab that message."

"But Henry's right. How would somebody even know it *was* a message?" Anna asked.

Hem plopped down on the bench. "You know who Ixchel is, right? The Mayan goddess of creativity?"

"Of course," Anna said. "The jaguar goddess."

José nodded. "And a symbol of the Silver Jaguar Society."

Henry flung his arm at the wall. "But there's zillions of notes up there. You're telling me somebody came in the window and happened to read that one and notice —"

"Yes." Hem ran his hand over the sea of greetings and sketches, notes and quotes. "Somebody who knew what he was looking for, too. A napkin . . . and a false attribution."

"Attri-what?" Henry asked. Hem threw around too many show-offy words.

"Attribution," Hem answered. "A quote or poem with the wrong name attached to it is always a society message. John Milton never wrote anything like that poem you saw," Hem said, rolling his eyes. "Any society member worth his salt would know that."

Worth his salt? Henry had no clue what that meant, but he was pretty sure Hem was being a jerk. "Are you saying we're not worth our salt? You know, we helped with two society missions before we even met you. We totally found the Star-Spangled Banner *and* the Jaguar Cup." He stalked across the room to look for his GamePrism.

"Well then, you're certainly the fellow for this job, aren't you?" Hem smirked.

"Maybe we can reconstruct the message." Anna jumped in, pulling out her notebook and a pen. "It started with, 'Ixchel's sons and daughters know . . . what's found below is . . .'"

"'What's sought above is found below,'" José corrected, then went on. "'Cizin's nature there beguiles, those who step and dare to smile, where time's a thief and dark eats light, where home is but eternal night . . . and . . .' I didn't read the end. Sorry."

"Dude, how'd you remember all that?" Henry stared at him.

José shrugged. "I memorize a lot of quotes and stuff. You get good at it after a while."

Anna was scribbling like crazy. "Cizin's nature . . ." she mumbled, then looked up at the others. "Who's Cizin?"

"Mayan god of death. He rules the underworld." Hem looked at Anna and Henry. "Anybody remember how it ends?"

Anna shook her head.

Henry thought hard. "Something with X marks the spot." That line had reminded him of his Treasure Quest game with Mad Ben the Pirate.

" 'Where all the past is laid to rest, the spot marked with imperfect X.' That's it!" Anna wrote it down and handed the notebook to Hem. "It's a riddle, right?"

"They always are." Hem frowned at the page, whispering the words to himself. For a while, they all watched him.

Finally, José yawned. "I guess we can show it to our parents when they get back." He looked at his watch.

"What time is it anyway?" Henry asked. When *were* the adults going to show up?

"A little after eleven," José answered. His voice was shaky, and Henry understood why. Were they supposed to go to bed in this weird bookstore by themselves? Why hadn't Aunt Lucinda called? And why hadn't his dad checked in? Was he *still* too busy at the hospital? That was hard to imagine . . . unless the baby wasn't doing well. As soon as Henry considered the possibility, his annoyed feeling turned to shame. What if something really was wrong?

"Oh!" Hem said suddenly, bringing Henry's thoughts back from the hospital. He held the notebook closer to his face, whispering the message again. ". . . who dare to *smile* . . ." He looked up at the others with his eyes wide. "I think this means they've got her!"

"Huh? Who's got who?" Henry asked.

"Mum . . . and the others." Hem tapped the page. "*They* stole the *Mona Lisa*. Not the Serpentine Princes."

"What?" Anna's mouth fell open. "They would never do that. They —"

"They certainly would if they felt it was the only way to keep her safe," Hem said.

"Dude . . ." Henry's jaw dropped. "You think your mom . . . and my aunt . . . and Anna's mom and the McGilligans actually *stole* the *Mona Lisa*?" If that was true, it was cooler than any video game Henry had ever played. But it was impossible. "No way could they get away with that."

"But there is," Hem whispered. "Mum said they have society members working in restoration at the Louvre. They could have pulled it off. If they felt there was a threat —"

"If there are society members working at the Louvre, why couldn't they *protect* her instead of stealing her?" Anna still looked horrified.

"Because they're not the only ones inside the Louvre," Hem said. "The Serpentine Princes have infiltrated half the museums in this city."

Henry nodded slowly. "That makes sense. In Storm the Castle —"

"This isn't a game, Henry!" Anna glared at him. "This whole idea is . . . stealing something to keep somebody else from stealing it first? I . . ." She stopped talking and let her words hang in the air. "Ohmygosh! This is just like . . ." She looked at Henry, and he knew exactly what she was thinking.

"Dude . . . it's the Jaguar Cup all over again," Henry said. A Silver Jaguar Society member in Costa Rica had stolen one of the society's most sacred artifacts, just as it was about to be loaned out for an international museum tour, because he thought it would only be safe if it could be kept in Latin America.

"And we know how that worked out," José said. "The cup was almost lost forever."

Anna shook her head. "We can't let them get the *Mona Lisa*!"

"I know." Hem's voice was calm, but his eyes looked wild. He pointed to the writing in Anna's notebook. "We need to figure this out, and we need to get there before —"

"Get *where*?" Henry interrupted. He felt like they'd jumped from level two to level sixteen in a game and missed all the directions.

"Get . . . wherever this is sending us." Hem held up the notebook. "I'm guessing . . ." He took a deep breath. "I'm guessing Mum and the others had to get rid of the painting quickly by stashing it somewhere . . . but now it's not safe."

Anna stared at the notebook. "You think this is trying to tell *us* how to find it? To save it?"

"Dude, you're not serious." If something like this showed up in one of Henry's video games, he and his friends would laugh it right off the screen. *Oh, look! A secret message . . . how convenient!*

"You don't get how serious this is." Hem's words came at Henry like bullets. "Maybe you haven't noticed, but our parents haven't come back. If they've taken the *Mona Lisa* . . . and then left us this" — he held up the notebook — "it's because something has gone desperately wrong, and we're the only ones who can get her to safety now."

Henry didn't know what to say. He looked at Anna and José. Anna's face looked as white as her notebook paper, and José's lower lip was trembling. Henry turned to Hem. "You really think that's what happened?"

Hem nodded. He didn't look full of himself anymore. He looked scared.

Henry took a shaky breath and tapped Anna's notebook. "Then let's try to figure this out." He tried to sound brave, confident. Maybe he couldn't do anything about the situation at the hospital back home. But he could do this. He could try — even though he had no idea where they were going, or who might be waiting when they got there.

THIRTEEN

.

"Where black is white is light as night . . ." Henry murmured, and felt a poke in his ribs.

"Hey!" José nudged him. "It's light out. We fell asleep again."

Henry sat up and groaned. They'd stayed awake almost all night, puzzling out bits of the poem. They'd worked as if it were the only thing on their minds, as if not one of them were watching the clock turn to midnight, then one, and two, without the grown-ups coming back. They'd huddled together, whispering through a thunderstorm that flashed and boomed in the courtyard outside the window and lit the gnomes' faces in creepy blue, until finally the rain died down and they couldn't stay awake any longer.

Now morning sunlight was coming through the window.

"They never came back," José said. "Unless they're downstairs. Maybe they didn't want to wake us."

"Maybe." But Henry knew in his gut it wasn't true. Without saying another word, he and José padded downstairs in their socks. They walked past stack after stack of old books, all the way through the empty store. Henry looked at José and shrugged, and they went back upstairs.

"Hey . . ." Henry stepped up to the bench where Hem had fallen asleep. He must have been drawing another map — it was flopped over him like a blanket and his fingers were smudged with ink. Henry gave him a shake. "It's morning . . . we should get back to work."

Henry found Anna still asleep, too, and tugged her notebook from her hands. She blinked awake, yawning. She'd copied the poem-message-thing onto a clean notebook page, spaced out, so they could make notes on it. Henry studied the marked-up lines again.

[Ixchel's sons and daughters know] ← Us?

What's sought above is found below↙ art? Below Louvre–City–Bookstore?

Underworld god
(Cizin's) nature there beguiles

Smile = Mona Lisa??

Those who step and dare to smile

clock?

Where time's a thief and (dark eats light,) ???

Where home is but eternal night. ← Graveyard?

Where all the past is laid to rest,
← Archives? Library?

The spot marked with imperfect X.
└ Like a treasure map?

~John Milton

"This kind of sounds like Hem's underground tunnels," Henry said.

"That's what I thought of first, but Mum had a fit the one time she found out I'd gone down." Hem looked over Henry's shoulder at the notebook page and shook his head. "Plus the tunnels go on forever — it'd be like finding a needle in a haystack. And it's all kinds of damp down there, too. No place for a fragile piece of art." He tapped the notebook page. "This has to mean something else."

Anna frowned at the page, then looked up at Hem. "Does Paris have any clocks, archives, libraries, or graveyards?"

"We've got lots of all of those things," Hem said, shaking his head. "Difficult to know where to even begin."

"The journey of a thousand miles starts with a single step," José said.

Henry made a face at him. "Who said that?"

"A Chinese philosopher named Lao-tzu."

"Yeah, well . . . I don't see him here helping us. A single step *where*?"

"If we were in Boston, the Old North Church would be perfect," Anna said. "It's got that old clock in the back and a lot of history. And an underground cemetery, kind of. Does Paris have a church with a crypt?"

"Notre-Dame." Hem shrugged. "But that's really more of a museum. Not the kind of place —"

"I think we should check it out." Anna was already closing her notebook and putting on her sweatshirt. "We have to start somewhere."

"We're not going to find anything." Hem sighed and rolled his eyes.

Henry folded his arms. "You got a better idea?"

Hem looked at the ceiling, thinking. "Maybe the basement of the Louvre," he said. "The foundation of the original palace is down there, and it's kind of dungeony, so it fits with 'found below' and where 'dark eats light.'"

"Then let's go there, too," José said. "The ancient Greek philosopher Euripides said, 'Leave no stone unturned.'" He looked at Henry. "But he's not here to help either."

"All right," Hem said, starting down the worn staircase. "We'll check Notre-Dame and then head for the Louvre basement. And then . . ."

"And then if we don't find anything," Anna said, following him down the stairs, "and our parents still aren't back, and your mom's still not answering her phone . . ." Her voice shook a little. "Then I think we should call the police because —"

"No." Hem stopped near the bottom step, so quickly Anna almost tripped over him. He turned back to face the rest of them. "We have a job to do. If we were supposed to get outside help, the message would have said so."

"Besides," Henry said, "Aunt Lucinda said only some special police group — Interpol or whatever — knows what's going on, and they sound all secret and important. If it was the sort of thing where we could just call them, I'm pretty sure she would have given us a number."

"Exactly," Hem said.

Henry wasn't sure he liked being on Hem's side, but he nodded.

José didn't look so certain. "You really think we're supposed to get involved in all this? As junior members of the society? Our parents always said that until we're eighteen —"

"They're not here, are they?" Hem's words hung in the air.

José swallowed hard. Henry caught Anna blinking fast, and his own heart started racing as they descended the last few stairs and passed through the empty bookstore toward the front door. Where *were* Aunt Lucinda and the other grown-ups?

"Look." Hem said. "Something must have gone wrong last night. If their mission had gone the way it was supposed to, they'd be back."

"And they're not." Henry took a deep breath. "So now this is up to us."

FOURTEEN

They left the bookstore and hurried down the bustling sidewalk and were halfway to Notre-Dame before it occurred to Henry that he didn't totally understand just *what* they were looking for. He edged closer to Hem. "Do you think this painting will still be in its frame? I mean, what should we be watching for when we get to the crypt?"

Hem led them across the street and hopped up onto the curb. "First, I don't think we're going to find anything here." He dodged a lady pushing a stroller. "Second, I have no idea how the piece was taken, if it'll be flat or packaged up in a box or what."

"Well . . ." Anna was jogging to keep up with Hem's long stride. "We'll just have to look for anything suspicious."

"Or not," Hem stopped abruptly at a stone wall and leaned over to point at a sign below.

CRYPTE ARCHEOLOGIQUE.

FERMÉ.

"Oh! That means closed," Anna said.

"Doesn't open for another twenty minutes," Hem added.

"Well, that's lame," Henry said. Seemed like any secret society member worth his salt would be able to find a way in to investigate. If this were a video game, they'd bust down a back door or rappel over a wall. But Henry looked around and couldn't find any secret entrances or ropes. He didn't even have his GamePrism. "Anything to do around here while we wait?"

"I'm going to take a nap." Hem shooed some pigeons off a bench and stretched out. "You can go see the cathedral if you want. That's open now." He waved his hand in the direction of the big church across the square, then put his fedora over his face.

"Oh, let's do that! I'll write a travel feature about it for my school paper." Anna pulled her notebook from her backpack.

"One thing." Hem lifted the hat from his face. "Watch for pickpockets." He wiggled his fingers. "They love you tourists."

Henry rolled his eyes and turned to José, who had been quiet all morning. "You coming?"

"Sure," José said as they started walking. As they

got closer to the huge cathedral, he turned to Henry, blinking fast. "Do you think they're okay?"

"Yeah." Henry had actually been trying not to think about Aunt Lucinda and the other grown-ups. "They've been on tons of other missions."

"And they're not alone," Anna added. "Mom says there are lots of society members in Paris, so even if something did go wrong, they'll . . . they'll get help."

José nodded, and they tagged onto one of the lines snaking toward the cathedral doors.

From across the square, Notre-Dame Cathedral had looked like a big letter *H* with the bottom space filled in. Henry thought it was cooler up close. If you looked straight up, these drooly stone gargoyle things stared down at you from the roof.

"Are you going in?" Anna nudged him from behind, and Henry realized the line had moved. He hurried through the cathedral's tall doorway. And stopped.

Anna did, too. "Ohh . . . it's beautiful," she whispered.

"Yeah." Henry stood still and took it all in, from the giant stone columns and arches to the brilliant stained-glass windows above the cross at the front of the church. It felt like staring into the Middle Ages.

"How old is this place?" he whispered, turning back to Anna and José. But they'd already wandered off. Anna was halfway up one of the aisles, scribbling in her notebook. On the other side of the church, José stood in front of a tall statue and a big, round wiry thing that held a bunch of little candles, all lit up.

Henry walked up to him. "Hey." He looked down at the unlit candle in José's hands. "What are you doing?"

"I was going to light a candle for my mom and dad," José said, "and your aunt and everybody, too. My grandma does it all the time at her church in Vermont." He paused. "It's supposed to . . . I don't know . . . help prayers work better, I guess. But I don't have two euros." He glanced up at a sign asking for the donation.

"Well," Henry said. He didn't know much about stuff like this. "We need help, so I think we gotta figure God won't mind." He peeked in the donation bowl, which was full of coins. "Besides, God's already doing pretty well this morning."

José nodded and moved to the next statue. "I wish there were a patron saint of kids whose parents might be missing."

"You guys!" Hem hissed from near the entrance. "The crypt's open. Let's go!"

"Just choose one," Henry said.

José lit a candle next to the Joan of Arc statue, then looked up at her. "We'd appreciate your help. Please look after our parents and Henry's aunt and bring them back safely."

José started toward the exit, but Henry paused and looked back at the statue. "If you could help out my dad and Bethany and the baby, too, that would be great," he whispered, and followed José out into the sunlight.

"What took you so long? Come on!" Hem started across the square. They dodged tourists, scared away a flock of pigeons, and hurried down the stairs to the entrance of the crypt. Hem led them past the tiny gift stand and some diorama displays, and along a railing that overlooked a pit full of old bricks and columns. They took a few steps down, and the air changed. It was cool and musty-damp, like rotten leaves.

Hem stopped to peer over another railing into the excavation pit but shook his head at the dirt and stones. "I'm not seeing anything."

"What *is* all this stuff?" Henry asked. It was nothing like the crypt of the Old North Church, with its carefully labeled tombs.

"History," Hem said impatiently, hurrying past some old oven-like thing. It reminded Henry of the place his dad used to take him for wood-fired pizza in Vermont before Bethany came along and they had to move. Hem rushed them past some more ruins. "The arches and stacks of rocks are from ancient Roman baths, but I don't think —"

"Hey, look!" Henry pointed through the bars of the railing, into the loose dirt next to one of the oven-things. There were footprints. And not from some crazy old fossilized ancient Roman. Modern foot-prints. "Those look like work boots."

Hem squatted down, peered into the shadows, then shrugged. "It could be a worker who was chang-ing a lightbulb or something."

"Maybe," Henry said. There were buttons on the sign to make different parts of the ruins light up. Henry pressed one. "But I don't think so, because look . . ." He pointed, moving his hand all over the pit as the lights changed. "Those prints aren't only where the lights are. They go all over the place, like some-body was looking for something."

"I doubt it." But Hem kept staring, frowning. Then he glanced up and down the empty walkway, climbed between the metal bars of the railing, and hopped into the archaeological site.

No alarms went off or anything, but Anna gasped. "Get back up here!"

José looked around. "No one seems overly con-cerned about his trespassing."

"What's he gonna do? Steal a rock?" Henry watched Hem bend down to inspect the footprints. He got on his hands and knees and started to crawl into the oven-thing. But he didn't get far.

"Anything in there?" Henry called down.

"No." Hem coughed, backing out of the archway. He stood up, returned to the walkway, and climbed back up, brushing old dirt off his knees and hands. "I don't think there was ever anything here." But he squatted again, squinted into the arch of the oven-thing, and frowned.

Henry did the same thing and understood. From the walkway, it looked like the arch might be a tunnel, like it might go way deeper than it did. Like maybe it was the kind of place you could hide something. "You think somebody else was looking for the *Mona Lisa* here?"

"Shhh!" Hem said. Then he nodded. "Yeah."

"Ohmygosh!" Anna's eyes were huge. "Whoever came in the window and took the napkin must be —"

"Shhh!" Hem headed for the neon exit sign, and they followed him up the stairs into the open square. "Well, we know one thing now." Hem folded his arms in front of him, as if he were cold, even though the sun was beating down. "We're not the only ones trying to solve this riddle."

José frowned. "But the painting wasn't there, so —"

"We got lucky. Whoever came here before us guessed wrong, too." Hem took a deep breath. "Next time, we need to get it right. Before someone else does."

"This is getting creepy," Anna said.

Henry nodded. It was like some weird multiplayer video game where you didn't even know who your opponent was. "So now what?"

Hem raised his eyebrows. "How do you feel about dungeons?"

FIFTEEN

The basement of the Louvre felt just like the crypt of Notre-Dame, all old stones and shadows.

"Is this a real dungeon?" Anna asked Hem, her pen poised over her notebook.

"Part of it. Come on . . ." He led them into a huge, circular room with crumbly walls. A modern wooden walkway snaked around the big center column of stones stacked upon stones. "The Louvre was originally built as a fortress in medieval times. This center tower was used as a prison and storehouse."

Henry eyeballed the tower. It looked pretty darn solid, and he didn't see any openings where somebody could hide a painting.

Hem's eyes scanned the curving stone walls. "There must be some nooks and crannies here where you could —" He jumped back from where he'd been standing, looked around wildly, ducked under the railing, and wiggled himself into the crawl space beneath the walkway.

Henry peered over the railing. "Did you find it?"

Anna and José hurried over, too, but Hem shook his head and held a finger to his lips. "Pretend I'm not here. Hurry! Walk that way" — he tipped his chin in the direction of the entrance — "and listen."

Henry looked toward the entrance. "Listen to what?" There was only a mom pushing a stroller through the entrance and, behind her, two guys with backpacks. "Who are those guys?"

"They're nobody. Just do it!" Hem squirmed deeper into the shadows.

Henry raised his eyebrows at José, who shrugged and started walking toward the entrance.

But there wasn't much to listen to. The mom was singing some quiet French baby song to her kid, and the two guys behind her were looking around. They looked like cartoon illustrations in a kids' book about opposites. One was the size of a sumo wrestler, with a square face and a black mustache that looked like the letter *M*. The other was tall and skinny with blond hair, pale skin, and wiry glasses. He wore jeans and dusty work boots. Henry followed those boots with his eyes. Could they have made the footprints in the Notre-Dame crypt?

"Stop staring," Anna whispered. She and José

started talking about their favorite paintings from upstairs. Henry pretended to be fascinated with a map on the wall. But when he snuck another glance at the men, they were looking at that center column of stone. The sumo wrestler gestured and then pushed up his shirtsleeves, and Henry gasped. A tattoo of a snake — the symbol that Vincent Goosen's thugs always had inked into their skin — slithered up the man's wrist and disappeared under his sleeve. These guys had to be Serpentine Princes!

The men started walking again, and Henry turned quickly back to his map, trying to listen over the thumping of his heart. The men were arguing in French.

"*Il n'y a rien ici!*"

"*Mais peut-être . . .*"

The first guy made a noise like he was hacking up phlegm. "*Non! J'avais raison. Vous êtes stupide. Allons au Panthéon!*"

Henry heard footsteps moving away from him, and when he dared to look, he saw the skinny man run right into Anna.

"*Excusez-moi,*" the man grumped.

"Oh. Um . . ." Anna looked up at the ceiling for a few seconds. "Umm . . . *de rien!*" she said finally. But they were already gone. "Oh." She looked at the empty doorway. "I can never remember French words fast enough."

"What did they say?" Hem asked as he slithered

out from the crawl space. He climbed back onto the walkway, brushing dusty rock crumbles off his pants.

"Dude, that big guy had a snake tattoo!" Henry's heart was still running wild in his chest. "They're Serpentine Prince members!"

"Obviously," Hem said.

"You *know* them?"

"I've seen their photos on Mum's computer."

Henry felt like he might explode. "You said they were nobody! You hid and you left us out here with them when you knew they were Serpentine Princes? What if they recognized us?"

Hem laughed. "Three junior society members who look like they're on a school field trip aren't exactly what the Serpentine Princes are trained to worry about." Hem waved his hand as if it were no big deal.

"Then why did *you* hide?" Henry glared at him.

"I'm a bit more high profile," Hem said, "what with my mum's position in the society here in Paris. I'm quite sure they would have recognized me."

Leave it to Hem to think he was some kind of society rock star.

"Anyway," Hem went on, "what did you hear?"

"They were arguing," José said.

"Saying what?" Hem looked excited.

"The first guy said, 'Blah blah blah,'" Henry said, still bristling. "And then the other guy said, 'Blah blah blah I have a raisin and you're stupid.'"

Hem blinked at him. "He said 'I have a *raisin*'?" He turned to Anna. "Don't you speak French?"

"Yes, but they were talking so fast! I only caught the very end. He said let's go . . . somewhere. It sounded like panty hose, but that can't be right."

Hem squinted at her. *"Allons au* . . . panty hose?"

Anna bit her lip. "Maybe it was panty-hone?"

"Panty-hone . . ." Hem said, and then his face lit up. "Panthéon! Of course . . . the Panthéon! Come on!"

Henry, Anna, and José ran to keep up with Hem as they hurried out of the Louvre, over the bridge, and through the city streets.

"So what is this Panthéon place?" Anna asked, trying to catch her breath, when traffic finally slowed them down.

"Used to be a church." Hem stopped at a corner. "Now it's a mausoleum, where our country's most distinguished citizens are entombed." As soon as there was a gap in traffic, he started running across the street. Henry tried to follow and almost got taken out by a moped.

When he caught up, he said, "Another crypt? Seriously?"

"Yes, there's a crypt. *And* a pendulum, and the message . . . time's a thief . . . I can't believe I didn't think of it sooner."

Anna grabbed Hem's arm. "Wait, what?"

"Time's a thief," Hem repeated as he led them past a little café. Henry looked longingly at a tray of ham-and-cheese baguettes behind the glass window. It had to be lunchtime, didn't it? Were they not going to eat until they found the stupid *Mona Lisa*?

"That time reference could very well be talking about the pendulum at the Panthéon." Hem ducked in front of a taxicab and jogged across another intersection, toward a huge building with tall stone pillars all across the front.

"The what at the who?" Henry was tired of all the dumb riddles. He was tired of this stupid, follow-Hem-because-he-knows-everything race through the city. He wanted a sandwich and a crepe and a nap.

"Just come on." Hem raced up the stairs and started toward the doorway. "None of this will matter if we don't get there first."

"No." Henry stepped in front of him. "You lied to us back at the Louvre. You've got us running all over the city. I can't understand a word anybody's saying. I almost got hit by a motorcycle, and —"

"It was only a moped," Hem interrupted.

"I don't care what it was!" The tourists hanging around on the steps were starting to stare, but Henry didn't care. "I'm not going anywhere else until I know what's going on."

"Then don't come. We can do without you quite nicely." Hem started to push past Henry.

This time, Anna stepped in front of him. "No. We're in this together until our parents come back. All of us. But Henry's right. You need to tell us what you're thinking so we can help."

"Fine." Hem sighed and plopped down on a step. Henry, Anna, and José lined up beside him — they looked like the pigeons perched on the edge of the bakery roof across the street — and leaned in to listen.

"The part of the message that said 'Where time's a thief' made me think of this place." Hem gestured toward the doors above them. "Foucault's pendulum is here and so is the Wagner clock," Hem said.

"Who are Foucault and Wagner?" Henry jumped in. "Those guys from the Louvre?"

"No." Hem rolled his eyes. "Foucault was a French physicist who created a pendulum clock model to prove that the Earth rotates. And Wagner was a clock-maker who came up with a particular kind of clock mechanism with gears and whatnot. Now can I finish?" Hem's voice had an edge. "You have to understand that the UX has a long history with the Panthéon. That's why this is so perfect."

"Wait . . ." Anna was having trouble keeping up in her notebook. "That's that Urban eXperiment group?"

"Right," Hem said. "The UX broke into the Panthéon a few years back, set up a secret workshop, and spent a year restoring the old Wagner clock."

"They break into buildings to *fix* stuff?" Henry couldn't help interrupting. That sounded kind of cool.

Hem nodded. "They're dedicated to restoring parts of Paris history that the government doesn't seem to care about anymore."

"They sound like the Silver Jaguar Society," Anna whispered.

"Indeed. There's a lot of overlap between the groups. So that's why I thought . . . time's a thief . . ." Hem looked at the doors. "I *wanted* to get here before those blokes from the Louvre."

It kind of made sense. *If* it was all true. "All right." Henry stood up. "Let's go."

Hem led them past the volunteer at the ticket desk into the lobby. The ceiling was high, vaulted, and billowy. The walls had huge murals and elaborate sculptures carved right into the stone, and in the middle of the floor was a big ring with numbers and lines, like a giant tape measure wrapped in a circle. Above it, a shiny golden ball swung back and forth on a long, straight wire. Henry tipped his head back to see where it was attached, at the very center of the domed ceiling overhead. A circle of tourists stood around it, watching the ball swing. It was kind of mesmerizing, like some giant hypnotist was holding the wire way up there.

They all watched the shiny ball swing back and forth until José broke the spell. "There's nowhere to hide anything here."

Anna looked around. "Where's the clock?"

Hem showed them a simple-looking old clock, way up high. There was no place to conceal a painting there either. "Let's go downstairs." He leaned in toward Henry, Anna, and José and whispered, "That's the only place you could stash anything, really."

They hurried downstairs and through a chilly room with a bunch of fancy, roped-off casket things. Each one had a statue of a guy in front of it.

"Oh!" José hurried over to one. "Voltaire is here? I love Voltaire!" He stared up at the statue, which was holding a notebook in one hand and some feathery pen in the other.

Henry turned to Anna. "He looks like the guy version of you, a few hundred years ago."

José made a face, as if Henry had offended the statue. "Don't you know who Voltaire is?" José struck a philosopher pose with his index finger sticking up in the air. "He said, 'Common sense is not so common,' and 'Every man is guilty of all the good he did not do.'"

"Whatever," Henry said, looking around. "Where'd Hem go?"

"Maybe over here?" Anna led them down a narrower hallway to the left.

"He probably ditched us. He said he'd rather be on his own," Henry said, following her.

"Well, that's not an option, because we're helping."

Anna stopped at a sign. "This must be a list of who's entombed here."

José read the names as if they were old friends. "Victor Hugo . . . Alexandre Dumas . . . Émile Zola . . ." It reminded Henry of the list of residents posted by the doorbells at their apartment building, only these tenants were all dead.

"Look who else is here." Henry pointed through the crowd, where Hem was wedged into one of the arched doorways. He must have climbed behind the iron railing that separated the tombs from the tourists, and he was tucked against the stone wall, peeking out.

"Good," Anna said, and started down the hallway.

But Henry grabbed her arm. "Wait a second . . ."

Henry, Anna, and José stayed back, watching as Hem leaned out his doorway a little. He tipped his head toward a cluster of people down the hall, his eyes cast up at the ceiling, listening.

"It's them!" Anna hissed, pointing. "Those Serpentine Prince guys from the Louvre!"

José stepped back as if he wanted to melt right into the stone wall, but Henry leaned forward to see.

The museum guys were standing in a cluster of people looking at whatever was in the next little room, but their attention wasn't on the tomb. They seemed to be arguing again.

"Doesn't look like they found anything here either." They were right back where they had started, and Henry was starting to feel like this stupid painting search would never end. It was like the worst video game ever, and they couldn't even get past level one. They needed a cheat code or something. Actually, what Henry really needed was lunch. He turned to Anna and José. "Let's go back to the bookstore."

But Anna held up her finger and looked past Henry, down the hall. Henry turned and saw the two Serpentine Prince guys walking away. Hem peeked out from his hiding spot, flung one long leg over the railing and then the other, and followed the guys toward the exit.

"Come on." Henry pointed back toward the big room with José's statue buddies. "Let's go this way and meet Hem outside. We can see what he has to say about all this." Henry couldn't help adding, "But I doubt we're going to hear the truth."

With all Hem's hiding and lying and eavesdropping, Henry had a bad feeling about him. A worse-than-usual feeling. And that was saying something.

SIXTEEN

"There you are!" Hem was just walking back into the lobby through one of the Panthéon's big open doors. "I went out to see if I'd missed you somehow."

"We're not the ones who ran off," Henry said, looking carefully at Hem. "So . . . did you find anything interesting?"

"Nah." Hem kicked at a brochure someone had dropped on the floor. "Another false alarm, I'm afraid. But I do have an idea. Let's go and we can talk."

"We saw those two guys from the Louvre again," Anna said as they went down the Panthéon steps outside. She started to say more, but Henry caught her eye and shook his head. He wanted to see if Hem would come clean about his hiding and listening.

"Really? Here?" Hem sounded surprised.

"They were downstairs," José said.

Anna frowned a little. "And we saw you —"

"We thought maybe you'd gone that way," Henry interrupted. He shot Anna a look. "Anyway, we were wandering around and saw those guys by one of the tombs."

"Wow." Hem nodded as if he were thinking.

Henry felt a puff of rage growing in his chest. He wanted to give Hem a good shove and say, "You are a big, fat liar with a stupid accent, and we are totally onto you now!" Instead, he nodded a little and said, "Weird, huh?"

Hem waved his hand in the air, jogged down the last few steps, and said, "Well, unless they were carrying the painting, I suppose they guessed wrong again, too. Let's get a bite to eat."

"But . . ." Anna began. Then Henry made big "shut-up" eyes at her, and she took the hint. "Yeah, okay. I'm hungry, too."

They walked down the street and alongside a big park that reminded Henry a little of Boston Common. This one was all fenced in with tall, pointy stakes.

Anna held on to two of the posts and peered between them at the trees and flower beds. "Nice park. Isn't it open to the public?"

"There's an entrance over there." Hem pointed down the sidewalk, then stopped walking and gazed at the row of markets across the street. "If you want to wait here" — he motioned to a bench along the park fence —"I'll pick up some cheese and baguettes."

After Hem left, Henry turned to Anna and José. "That guy is totally hiding something."

"Maybe." José frowned thoughtfully and wandered over to the fence by the park.

"'Maybe' nothing." Henry kicked at the sidewalk. "He's all 'Don't tell Ursa anything. . . . What if she's the traitor?' You know what? I betcha Hem's the one feeding information to the Serpentine Princes. He's the one who's lying all over the place. He's the one who —"

"Henry, that's ridiculous." Anna said. "You're being hungry and grumpy." She climbed up on the lower concrete part of the fence, holding on to the rails to steady herself, and walked along as if it were a balance beam.

"No, I'm not," Henry said, even though he was both of those things. "Hem lied about those guys from the Louvre. Why else would he do that?"

"Well . . ." Anna stepped down from the ledge, came back to the bench, and plunked herself down. "I think we should ask him."

"He'll only lie again." Henry looked across the street to the market, where Hem stood at the counter with his cell phone pressed to his ear. "I mean, look at him. We've heard nothing from your parents or Aunt

Lucinda, and he's over there making secret phone calls, and —"

"He's over there getting us food because you keep whining."

"Hey, you guys?" José called from the fence.

"What?" Henry grumped.

"I think I see Hem's mom."

"What?" Anna and Henry flew across the sidewalk and attached themselves to the iron fence as if they were made of magnets.

"Look." José pointed toward a woman with curly blond hair, walking down a path covered in fallen leaves. "Doesn't that look like Miranda?" She was facing away from them, but then she turned.

Anna gasped. "It *is* her! That's totally her!"

"Shouldn't our parents be with her?" José asked, still staring through the bars.

Henry looked, too. Hem's mom was by herself. She kept walking until she disappeared around a bend in the path.

"Come on." Henry hurried along the fence, then stopped again to look through. "There she is." Hem's mom was leaning against a thick tree trunk, staring at her phone. Every few seconds, she'd look up and glance around.

"I think she's waiting for someone," José said.

"We should call her." Anna climbed back up on

the concrete ledge, but José tugged her sleeve, and she came back down.

"What if she's undercover?" he asked.

"Yeah, but — oh! She's waving to somebody. There she goes!" Anna climbed back up and pressed her face against the bars.

"Who'd she wave to?" Henry climbed up, too, but he couldn't see Miranda anymore.

"I couldn't tell." Anna jumped down. "But she's obviously okay, and she has her phone, so when Hem gets back, I think we should —"

"Don't say anything to Hem. Not yet," Henry told them, and took off running down the street.

"What are you doing?" Anna yelled after him.

"Be right back," Henry hollered over his shoulder, and darted through a crowd of school kids in blue shirts. He raced along the sidewalk, found the park entrance, and ran down a walkway parallel to the street, heading back to the area where they'd seen Hem's mom.

Henry scanned the path ahead of him as he ran, but it was mostly full of college kids with backpacks and moms pushing kids in strollers. No Miranda.

Who was she meeting? If it was Aunt Lucinda, Henry wanted to see her. Even if she wasn't done with the mission, he wanted to talk to her and see if she'd heard from his dad. He wanted to know she was coming back to get him and not leaving him with stupid Hem forever. And besides that, he wanted to know why Aunt Lucinda and Miranda couldn't go fetch their own dumb painting if they had time to be hanging out in a park.

Henry slowed down a little. He was so hungry and out of breath he couldn't keep up with his own ideas anymore. Why had the kids even gone out looking for the *Mona Lisa*? How was it their job? Henry couldn't even remember why Hem had been so sure they were supposed to do this. The more he thought, the more it sounded like an incredibly dumb idea — send a bunch of kids out into a city most of them don't know, where they don't speak the language, and expect them to find the most famous painting ever stolen from anywhere? If this were a video game, it would get awful reviews.

Henry stopped and bent down to catch his breath. He wiped his sweaty nose with his sleeve and looked around. There was no sign of Miranda, and he didn't even know where he was anymore. He wished he had one of Hem's maps to follow.

There was a fountain up ahead, near the fence. Henry headed that way to see if he was anywhere near where Anna and José were waiting.

And that's when he saw her.

Hem's mom stood next to one of the flowerpots that lined the fountain's reflecting pool, talking to someone whose face Henry couldn't see. The man stood in the shadow of a heart-shaped bush, facing the fountain, away from Henry. It definitely wasn't José's dad; this guy was taller and more muscular.

Henry looped a wide circle around the fountain. He tried to look like a French student just chilling out in the park, but his heart was racing.

He couldn't see much more from the other side of the reflecting pool. Miranda was facing away from Henry now, and the guy was mostly hidden in the heart bush. His orange shirt stood out, but his features were hidden in leaves and shadows. Henry was going to have to get closer.

The big flowerpots that lined the reflecting pool all sat on thick stone pillars. Henry dropped to his knees and crouched behind one.

He peeked out to make sure no one was watching. Then he ran all crouched over to the next pillar and hunched down.

Pillar by pillar — *crouch* — *race* — *hide* — Henry made his way to the front of the fountain, where rushing water drowned out the sound of his sneakers thumping the concrete. He hid behind the last pillar and looked up at the sculpture looming over him.

A man and woman carved in light gray stone were sprawled out on a little island. Next to them was a big boulder, and on top of that was a ginormous, ugly, coppery-greenish giant who looked like he was about to bash their brains in.

Henry looked away from the sculpture and poked his head out from behind the pillar a tiny bit so he could look across the reflecting pool to where Miranda and that guy were talking.

Henry was closer now — close enough to count the tangly rings of curls on the back of Miranda's head — but he still couldn't see the guy's face.

Finally, Miranda made a big gesture with her hands and stepped to the side.

When Henry saw the man's face, he felt a chill of recognition that made his stomach twist and his neck prickle.

The man had Vincent Goosen's thin, greasy hair and Vincent Goosen's pitch-black mustache.

He had piercing dark eyes that looked past Miranda as he spoke to her. Those eyes scanned the walkways, darted from tourist to student to stray dog. Then they landed on Henry.

Miranda turned and saw Henry, too. She said something to the man, and he lurched forward, stumbling through the heart-shaped bush. He barked something in French, leaped over the fence, and splashed through the fountain in big rubber boots.

Henry scrambled to his feet and ran.

SEVENTEEN

Henry tore down the walkway alongside the fountain, away from the stone couple and the big guy leering over them. He didn't look back at the real live big guy about to crush him. He didn't need to; he could hear from the man's out-of-breath shouting that he was getting closer.

When Henry reached the end of the fountain pool, the trail split. Going right would take him back the way he'd come, to that open gate so he could return to the street. He paused for a split second, then darted left. As much as he hated being trapped inside the fenced-in park with this guy, going back would mean running right past Miranda, and who knew which side she was on now?

Henry heard another gruff shout behind him and veered onto a more crowded path. Couples holding hands lurched out of his way as he raced down the walkway, pumping his legs, forcing himself to go faster, faster.

He had no idea where he was anymore; all that mattered was putting space between him and — who *was* the man Miranda met by the fountain? He *looked* like Vincent Goosen, but —

It didn't matter. He had to keep moving. He dodged his way through a pack of students holding greasy paper bags and caught a whiff of something spicy and fried. He wished he'd eaten something — anything — that would have given him more energy.

The walkway curved and ran parallel to some big fancy building on Henry's right. Another path led to a big open area with a sparkling pond in the center. Henry ran that way and imagined sucking in a big gulp of that cool water. His throat ached. He tried to swallow, but his mouth was all sticky and dry. It was impossible to run as fast through the crowds here. Every few seconds, it felt like somebody stopped right in front of him to snap photos of a kid poking a little sailboat out onto the pond.

Henry had circled halfway around the pond when he realized no one was shouting anymore. Had the guy given up? Henry threw a glance over his shoulder and didn't see anyone chasing him. He slowed down and watched for a few seconds more, and finally, when there was no sign of the man's orange shirt,

Henry stopped and scanned the crowd around the fountain.

The sidewalk was mobbed with toy boat sailors of all ages. Couples strolled hand in hand, shuffling through the crunchy leaves, and old men sat at tables along the sidewalk, sliding chess pieces across boards, flipping timers.

Henry's breathing had finally started to slow when he spotted the man in the orange shirt on the other side of the pond. The man had stopped running. He was doubled over, hands on his knees, catching his breath. At least Henry had managed to put some space between them.

Henry slipped behind one of the chess tables and squatted down. One of the old men was so focused on the board he didn't even notice, but the other glared and muttered something Henry didn't understand.

"Sorry," Henry said.

The man grouched a little more, but then his opponent flipped the timer and he turned back to the game. Henry squatted behind the table, peering through the knights and pawns.

The man in the orange shirt stood up and wiped his sweaty red face with his sleeve. He scanned the crowd, his dark eyes tracing the sidewalk all around the pond. Henry knew those eyes. It had to be Vincent Goosen.

The man unbuttoned the top of his shirt and tugged open the collar. Henry stared at his neck, waiting for him to expose the tattoo that curled around his throat.

But it wasn't there.

"Ay-sheck!" one of the men at the chess table exclaimed. Henry glanced up. His head was spinning. He hoped that wasn't checkmate. He needed time to think. The man across the pond ran his hand along his neck, then turned his head from side to side.

There was definitely no tattoo.

Back at the fountain with the statues, when Miranda had moved so quickly to one side and the man's face flashed at Henry, he'd been so sure it was Vincent Goosen.

But it couldn't be.

Because a thick green-and-black serpent tattoo snaked up from Vincent Goosen's chest and slithered around his neck. Henry had seen it in photos and then last year in real life when they encountered Goosen in Costa Rica. All the Serpentine Princes had the tattoo somewhere, but Goosen's was the biggest, the most prominent. It was impossible to miss.

And this man didn't have it, so who *was* he? Henry stared across the rippling water and looked more closely. Knowing now that it couldn't be Vincent Goosen, Henry realized this man's build was wider and thicker than Goosen's wiry frame. And his face . . . his face looked less worn though just as fierce.

"His son," Henry whispered to himself. How could he have forgotten? The Silver Jaguar Society thought this latest heist might be Goosen's attempt to get his son out of prison. Had Goosen already brokered some kind of deal? Or had his son managed to escape somehow? If this was actually —

"Ay-sheck-ay-mat!" one of the old men shouted, and stood up from the table, reaching his hand across toward his opponent. Then they both glared down at Henry.

"Sorry . . . I just . . ." Henry looked up at the men, than glanced back to find Goosen — no, wait . . . Goosen's son?

Whoever it was, the man was gone.

Henry sprang to his feet in a panic, and chess pieces flew.

The old men threw their hands in the air, hollering.

And then another voice cut through the yelling and the kids laughing. Henry turned toward the sound and saw the man with the orange shirt running straight for him.

EIGHTEEN

Henry stumbled through the scattered chess pieces, found a gap in the crowd, and took off. He raced around the pond, dodging old ladies and jumping over strollers. He glanced over his shoulder just in time to see the man in the orange shirt topple a small, round table, spilling drinks onto the two women sitting there. The man didn't pause to apologize. He didn't slow down. His eyes were fixed on Henry, and he was gaining ground.

Henry zigzagged through the maze of flower beds surrounding the pond and ducked onto another pathway. If he made enough quick turns, maybe he could lose the guy.

Henry ran past a bunch of statues and veered onto a narrower path that turned to his right. But the man was still behind him — getting closer.

Henry sucked in big gulps of air and tried to go faster, but he didn't know how long he could keep this up. Where was his energy booster? In video games, all you had to do was look for the sparkling power pill, scoop it up, and you'd be good for another ten minutes.

But it didn't work that way when a bad guy was chasing you in real life. Henry's only hope was getting lost in a crowd. Up ahead, he could see a big group of moms and kids, so he put on a burst of speed and raced toward them.

The moms were loading the kids onto an old-fashioned carousel, with painted horses and lions and little cars that rode in circles. Before Henry got there, the carousel started up, making slow rotations, then picking up speed. He knew if he tried to go in the regular entrance, the ticket-taker guy would stop him. He'd be stuck outside the green fence with whoever was chasing him.

So Henry raced past the break in the low green wire fence that surrounded the carousel. He looked back to watch the ticket guy, and when the man looked the other way, Henry turned and flung himself sideways over the low fence.

His shoulder caught the edge of a wooden bench before he thumped hard onto the concrete. His arm throbbed, but he rolled to his feet and ran for the carousel. Maybe if he got to the other side . . .

Henry paused for a split second and glanced over his shoulder. The man in the orange shirt was stopped at the fence, hollering something at the ticket guy, waving his arms like crazy.

Henry jumped onto the merry-go-round platform and leaped onto a black horse. Then he slid off again and started running around the circle between two rows of horses.

"Hey! You have to stay on your animal!" shouted a little girl clinging to the neck of her giraffe. She had an accent like Hem's — were British people *all* that bossy?

Henry ran past the girl, dodged two teenagers riding sidesaddle on horses, and almost crashed into a toddler on an elephant, but he didn't stop.

The parents on the benches were starting to point, and Henry couldn't see where the man in the orange shirt was anymore. This was his chance. He lunged between two outside horses and jumped from the carousel. He stumbled but didn't fall. He kept going, took a running leap over the fence on the other side, and found another fence — a higher one — circling an enormous playground. It was mobbed with swarming kids, full of noisy chaos. It might be Henry's best chance to disappear.

The fence was too high to jump but easy to climb. Henry jammed his sneaker toe in one of the openings, hoisted himself up, and swung a leg over the top.

"Ay!" a deep voice shouted. Henry's heart flew into his throat, but when he turned, he saw that the man shouting wore a green parks department vest. He was hollering in French, pointing to a sign near the fence:

ENTREE 7€

Henry didn't have seven dollars or seven euros or seven anythings, and there was no time to explain. He jumped down, stumbled through a sandbox full of dump trucks, ducked under a climbing thing that looked like a miniature Eiffel Tower, and raced up the steps to a big slide and jungle-gym structure.

At the top, he dove into a tunnel, sat down, and leaned back against a cool wooden post, panting.

"Allons-y!" barked a shrill voice in Henry's ear. He looked up and saw a grubby-faced five- or six-year-old kid crouched in the tunnel with his arms crossed and a snotty look on his face. He gestured for Henry to get moving.

"Go ahead." Henry pulled in his legs so the kid could crawl past and go down the slide. But he knew he couldn't stay huddled in the friendly yellow-and-orange jungle gym forever. He took a deep breath and leaned forward to look out the slide hole.

The park was bursting with activity, and play-ground fun sounded pretty much the same in any language. For a few seconds, Henry listened and watched. A mom lifted a toddler onto a swing. A dad raced a little girl around the sandbox.

Henry felt a lumpy knot of resentment growing in his chest. He wished he could go down the slide and play, too. No, what he really wanted was to go home to Boston and his dad. How did he even get into this mess? He'd never asked to be part of the Silver Jaguar Society. He didn't even like art. Why couldn't somebody else protect it and get chased around?

"*Allons-y!*" The bossy kid was back. And he was right. Henry couldn't hide forever.

Henry looked out from the slide. There was no sign of the man in the orange shirt, so he wiggled himself around, slid down, and turned in a circle, searching the crowd.

The guy who had been chasing him was gone.

Henry made his way to the playground exit and started walking down another tree-lined path. He needed to find his way to that perimeter fence and follow it until he could get back out to the street.

Henry started jogging. As he approached an intersection of two paths, he heard footsteps coming quickly in his direction.

Before Henry could duck into the trees or hide or even think, a man burst into the intersection, red faced and wild-eyed.

It was him.

"Gah!" Henry took off the other way. The path was closed in with bushes on both sides and seemed to loop in circles. No matter how far Henry ran, he raced past the same weird statue over and over again — some guy with a regular head and a big, tall concrete block for a body. Maybe that was what happened to people who got stuck in this stupid loop — their legs turned to stone and then pigeons landed on them and pooped on their heads.

Henry glanced back. The guy chasing him never stopped, no matter how tired and sweaty he looked. He was like the super-powered brain eaters in Zombie-Robot Apocalypse.

Henry raced around another loopy curve and finally found himself on a path that went straight. Up ahead — *yes*! It opened up onto the street.

Henry felt like he'd finally found the power pill. His legs burned, but he pushed himself to go faster, faster, until he flew out of the trees, through a park gate and onto the sidewalk. Now where could he go?

Into a building? The man would follow him, Henry was sure of that.

Way down the street, Henry spotted a police car, its lights flashing behind a pulled-over truck, and he thought about running there — only Aunt Lucinda had given him the impression that might not be safe either. Not unless it was Interpol, or whatever that one agency working with the Silver Jaguar Society was called.

Henry didn't know if he could run much farther, but he couldn't stay here. He looked up and down the busy street and saw a familiar metal arch with a yellow sign at the center: METROPOLITAIN.

The Métro! Henry remembered the image of another man racing for the yellow sign, disappearing down the stairs into the dark. The purse thief they'd seen — and what had Hem said about the tunnels? *It's easy to disappear down there.*

Henry raced down the steps and found himself squeezed into a mob of men and women with briefcases. He ducked under a turnstile and pushed through the crowd just as a train pulled up to the platform.

Should he get on? Henry was pretty sure that wasn't how the purse snatcher had disappeared. Hem said thieves jumped the tracks and escaped down the tunnels, but no way was Henry about to try that after how fast this train had come flying down the tracks. But he couldn't get trapped on that train either. Who knew where he might end up? The crowd was pushing forward, practically carrying Henry up to the edge of the tracks. He pushed back, wiggling through bodies, ducking under elbows, until he saw a row of chairs along the wall with a skinny silver trash can nearby.

It was a crummy hiding place, but Henry had to get out of this crowd, or he'd be carried along onto the train. He shoved through the mob, crouched behind that trash can, tried to think skinny-invisible thoughts, and waited.

Henry peeked out. The mass of bodies was shrinking as the train took them in, like a puddle of water getting sucked up by a sponge. A few stragglers raced across the open space on the platform as the doors started to close, and they opened again. An Asian couple jumped on board the train, laughing, and after them — yes!

Henry ducked back behind the garbage can. *Leave. Just leave*, he thought. He didn't dare look again until he heard the train start to pull away, and only then did he peek out and see the man in the orange shirt. His face was pressed right up to the window so Henry could see every detail — the man's slick black hair, his perfectly trimmed mustache, and his furious eyes — as the train sped away.

NINETEEN

"Hey! We were about to give up on you!" Hem called down the street as Henry turned the corner that brought him back to the others.

"Yeah . . ." Henry glanced at Anna and José. Had they told Hem about seeing his mom? "I got a little lost in the park."

Hem laughed his condescending laugh. "I don't suppose you caught up with my mum in there?"

"What?" Henry's eyes darted to Anna and José — then back to Hem. They must have told him. "I . . . no. We thought we might have seen her, but I couldn't find her."

Henry might have imagined it, but he thought a flash of relief passed over Hem's face. He waited to see what Hem would say.

But Anna jumped in. "It wasn't Miranda." She

sounded sure of herself. "She just called Hem when he was coming out of the shop. She's on her way into a society meeting near the . . . Troca-something." She looked at Hem.

"Trocadéro," he said, pointing up the street. "Way up by the Eiffel Tower. So unless she's learned to apparate" — He smirked at José, who smiled back. *Probably some dumb Harry Potter joke*, Henry thought. — "it was someone else you spotted in the park. Mum'll be pleased to know she has a doppelgänger."

Anna tipped her head. "Doppelgänger?"

"A look-alike," Hem said, grinning. "It's a German word." He looked down at the paper bag in his hand and handed it to Henry. "You want lunch?"

Henry's stomach was begging for whatever had made the grease marks on the brown paper, but he hesitated. Hem was lying — flat-out lying. But food from a liar was better than nothing. Henry took the bag, pulled out a baguette stuffed with ham and cheese, and took a bite.

"Okay if we walk while you eat?" Hem started down the street without waiting for Henry's answer.

Henry turned to follow him and saw the towering roof of the Panthéon up ahead. "Hey! Isn't this the wrong way?" Henry had gotten all kinds of turned around in the park, but he knew the bookstore was in the other direction.

"No," Hem said, not even slowing down.

"But the bookstore's back there." Henry stopped.

So did José. "I think you're right. Shouldn't we be heading back?" he called up to Hem.

Hem stopped and turned to face them. "The bookstore is back that way, but there's one more place I want to —"

"No." Henry's stomach twisted. "No way."

"But —"

"No!" Henry wheeled around and started walking away, but then he realized he couldn't leave Anna and José. They didn't know Hem was lying. They didn't know about Miranda and Goosen's son or whoever it was. Who knew where Hem might be planning to lead them? Henry turned back and caught up with them. "You guys, come on. We should go back."

Anna looked at Hem. "Where are we going? How far is it?"

Hem shrugged. "Just a . . . museum I want to check. It's not far at all. Maybe a twenty-minute walk."

"That's not bad." Anna turned to Henry.

"No. We need to go back." Henry's heart thudded in his chest. He had to get Anna and José alone. They needed to know they couldn't trust Hem anymore.

"Come on, mate." Hem reached out to put a hand on Henry's shoulder.

Henry jerked away. "Get away from me!" His voice came out too loud, too scared. *Keep cool*, Henry thought, *or Hem will know something's up*. He looked around. They weren't too far from the sandwich shop. "I . . . sorry, man. I'm really tired. And thirsty, and I can't order in French. Any chance you'd run back and get me something to drink? Then I might be up for another walk."

"Oh, sure! Be right back, then." Hem started jogging toward the café.

Henry motioned for Anna and José to come close, and he told them everything that had happened in the park.

"You're certain it was Goosen's son?" José asked.

"It had to be. He looked just like Goosen, only without the tattoo."

"But one of his sons is in prison — we know that — and the other's been missing for years." Anna frowned. "Are you sure the woman was Miranda? Maybe Hem's right and it was a doppelgänger."

"A person who just *happened* to look exactly like Hem's mom talking to a person who just *happened* to look like Vincent Goosen? And that person happened to feel like chasing my butt all over the park? Doppel-*not!*"

"That would be quite a stretch." José's eyes shot past Henry toward the storefront. "Here he comes. How shall we handle this?"

"I'm not going anywhere else with that guy," Henry whispered.

"No . . . you're right," Anna said. "It's not safe until we know more. We'll tell him we're tired, and we're going back, and then when we get to the bookstore, we can do a little research and try to find out more about —"

"I got two waters and two Cokes," Hem announced, juggling the bottles in his arms. "Who wants what?"

Henry took a Coke, and José and Anna took water.

"Listen," Henry said, "we're going back."

Hem's face fell for a second, but then it filled with determination. "No, really . . . you have to come with me. I'm sure I've got it this time, and I need you because —"

"We don't have to do anything." Henry's voice was louder than he meant it to be.

"Maybe later," Anna said. "We're exhausted. And I want to see if there's been any word from our parents."

"I swear this won't take long. It's important. Trust me, okay?"

Henry couldn't help it. He let out a sharp scoff.

Hem's eyes fell on Henry, then moved to Anna and José, searching their faces. He apparently didn't like what he saw. "Fine." Hem wheeled around and started down the street, away from where he said he'd wanted to go.

"Where are you going?" Anna called after him.

"Don't worry about it." Hem flung the words over his shoulder. "I'm sure Henry can help you find your way back to the shop."

Henry tried. But he made a bunch of wrong turns on streets that ran along the park, so they wandered in circles half the afternoon.

Finally, Anna figured out how to ask for directions in French. She jumped in front of a lady with a bunch of shopping bags. *"Bonjour! Où est la Seine?"*

The lady raised one eyebrow, pointed, and said, "Go straight and you'll run right into it."

Anna bristled as they started walking again. "How did she know I spoke English?"

"These French people are like wizards," José said. "They can tell a Muggle a mile away."

Finally, they got to the river and turned the corner, and there was the green-and-yellow bookshop. Henry wanted to kiss it, and he didn't even like books all that much.

"Hey, is that Hem?" José stood on the sidewalk, pointing to a doorway next to the bookstore, just as Hem stepped away from it. He walked down the sidewalk and across the street.

"Looks like him. Unless it's his doppel-whatever." Henry watched as Hem or his double went over the bridge and hurried past Notre-Dame. "Let's follow him."

Hem wasn't walking all that fast. Once he even looked over his shoulder as if he knew someone might be following him, and Henry, Anna, and José ducked behind tourists to hide. But Hem kept walking, in no hurry at all. After a few blocks, he turned down an alley, then stopped and crouched down in the middle of the street.

"If a bus comes, he's getting squashed," Henry whispered from behind the bicycle rack where they were hiding.

"Shh." Anna peered between the spokes of a blue-and-yellow bike. "He's got a big stick or something."

Henry squinted. "It's a crowbar." Hem was using it to pry something up from the street. "It looks like a manhole cover. I bet he's going into one of those underground tunnels!"

Sure enough, Hem lifted the round metal cover from the street, rolled it to one side, climbed down the hole, and carefully dragged the cover back over the hole before he disappeared.

Anna stood up. "Should we follow him?"

Henry shook his head. "Uh-uh. What if it's a trap? He kind of looked like he wanted to be followed. I say we go back to the store and then figure out what to do."

So they walked back to Shakespeare and Company, waved to Ursa at the checkout counter, wound their way through customers browsing in the back room, and climbed the stairs to the children's section.

Henry plopped down on his bench, exhausted. He jumped about a mile when Anna lunged at him.

"It's another one!" She reached over his head and pulled a green napkin from the bulletin board.

She held it up, and José leaned in to see. "A message?"

"Hard to say," Henry said. "It's in French."

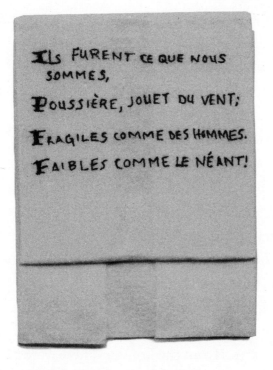

Anna couldn't read it — except to report that *ils* meant *they* and *fragile* probably meant *fragile* — so they went downstairs to the computer at the checkout counter. Ursa was happy to let them use it "for Anna's school assignment," so Anna typed the poem into a website she used for homework sometimes and hit "Translate."

"Here we go!" She clapped her hands together and read, "They were what we are. Dust, a plaything of the wind. Fragile as men — see! I was right about it meaning fragile! — Feeble as nothing." She nodded, pleased with herself.

"Huh." These poems made Henry's head hurt.

"Does it say who wrote it?" José asked.

Anna looked at the napkin. "Nope."

"Try pasting the whole poem into the search engine," José said. "That's what I do when I'm unsure of the attribution of a quote I want to put in my notebook."

Anna tried that. "These websites are all in French." She sighed. "No, wait! Here's one in English." She clicked on one of the results.

When the page loaded, she scrolled through a bunch of pictures of bridges and mountains and people kayaking. "Looks like somebody's travel journal," she said, speeding up. "Oh, wait! Here's Paris . . ."

Henry recognized Notre-Dame and one of the naked statues from the Louvre. There were a bunch of really dark pictures and then some writing. "Slow down! I think that's it!"

The poem was there, along with the translation they'd found. "It doesn't say who wrote it," Anna scrolled back up through the dark pictures. "But look . . . it's engraved on the plaque in this picture. Now we need to figure out where this is . . . someplace with lots of dark stone walls." She scrolled through the rest of the photos.

"Hold on. Are those . . ." Henry leaned in to the computer. He was pretty sure he was seeing wrong.

No. He wasn't.

His stomach turned, just as Anna and José gasped.

Not stone walls.

Bone walls.

"Oh . . ." Anna scrolled slowly back through the pictures. There were skulls and long leg bones. Bones piled on bones piled on bones. "What kind of place is this?"

"Some messed-up cemetery?" Henry couldn't believe it was real.

Anna found what the traveler had written in her journal. "She says it's called the Catacombes de Paris. They moved six million of Paris's dead to these old stone quarries when the cemeteries were overflowing in the 1700s. I guess it's like a tourist attraction now."

José stared at the screen and whispered the translation. "'They were what we are. Dust, a plaything of the wind. Fragile as men. Feeble as nothing.'" He swallowed hard. "Now it makes sense."

"So . . . the cemeteries were full" — Henry couldn't stop staring at the bones — "and they decided to dig up the bones and use them to build walls with freaky poems on them? These French people are seriously messed up."

"Six million people's bones . . ." José whispered.

Anna nodded. "And one stolen painting. This must be where they hid it!" She thought for a few seconds, and then gave a little jump. "Ohmygosh . . . remember in Boston when they were talking about 'looking for her in the tunnels'? They didn't mean the Isabella Stewart Gardner portrait; they must have been talking about their plans for the *Mona Lisa!*"

Anna started pacing back and forth. "I can't believe we didn't figure this out before. I mean, we didn't know this place existed or we would have, but . . . it totally fits the poem, too. What's sought above is found below? Where dark eats light and home is but eternal night? And let's see something. . . ." She went back to the computer.

"But Hem said it's all damp down there." José's voice wobbled. "And he said his mom —"

"Hem's a liar." Henry crossed his arms.

"And besides," Anna said, scrolling through pictures on the computer, "this isn't the illegal part of the tunnels where it's all wet. It's like a museum. And . . . ohmygosh, look!"

Henry and José leaned forward. On the screen was a skull — its hollowed-out eyes seemed to be looking right into Henry's — above two bones making a cross.

"The spot marked with imperfect X," José whispered. "You're right." He swallowed hard. "It fits the poem exactly."

"That X looks perfect to me." Henry really didn't want to hang around all those bones.

But Anna was already typing again.

"What are you doing?" Henry was afraid he already knew the answer.

"Looking up directions."

Henry glanced at the clock on the wall. "Dude, it's getting dark. I am not going into some freaky bone tunnel to look for a painting."

"Of course not," Anna said.

Henry felt a little of the doom feeling lift from his heart. "Really?"

"Not tonight. The travel journal lady said you have to get there early in the morning or the line's too long." She clicked a button and smiled when the printer under the cash register started spitting out a map.

"All set with your homework?" Ursa asked, looking over Anna's shoulder.

"Yes, thanks!" Anna grabbed her printed map and started for the stairs. "Come on, you guys." She motioned for Henry and José to follow her. "We need to get an early start tomorrow."

TWENTY

Hem never came back to the store that night. Ursa offered to stay when the last customer left a little before eleven, but otherwise, she didn't seem concerned that the adults hadn't come back. "These missions can be so unpredictable," she said, "but I'm sure you know that. Are you certain you won't want me to keep you company?"

"No, we'll be fine. We're used to this," Anna lied.

"Why'd you tell her that?" Henry watched through the window as Ursa walked toward the subway. With Aunt Lucinda and everyone gone, it would have been nice to feel like somebody was watching out for them.

"Because," Anna said, flipping open her notebook, "if Ursa's here in the morning, she'll want to know where we're going and she'll probably tell us we can't go because we're *junior* members" — Anna rolled her eyes — "and then how are we going to find the *Mona Lisa*?"

"Did you ever think maybe we *shouldn't* go?" José asked.

"José!" Anna's mouth hung open. "Aren't you the one who said, 'The test of any man lies in action'?"

"No, that was Pinhead," Henry said.

"Pindar. The Greek poet," José corrected. "Who also said, 'Learn what you are and be such.'"

"And you are . . . ?" Anna raised her eyebrows.

"Kind of afraid of that Catacombs place," he admitted.

"José, it's open to the public. How scary can it be?"

José sighed. "Okay. I suppose we'd better try to get some rest."

That was easier said than done. Henry tossed and turned on his stupid little bench all night. Once, he woke up shivering and thought he felt a breeze, but then he dozed off and it was warmer when he woke up again. It felt like he'd barely slept when somebody started poking him in the shoulder.

"Henry, wake up!"

Henry opened his eyes. "Seriously?" Early morning sun lit Anna's impatient face. "What time is it?"

"Ten after six. But it's a long walk, and I want to be

there early so we can get in first, because once it fills up with school groups and tourists it's going to be impossible to get anything done." She said all this as if she rescued paintings from underground grave-yards all the time and knew exactly how to do it.

"What's that?" Anna shoved past Henry, reached for something yellow on the bulletin board behind him, and gasped. "It's another napkin! With a map! Was this here last night?"

"I don't think so." Henry had been totally wiped out, though. Would he have noticed? "Maybe."

"Is it one of Hem's?" José came into the room. The back of his hair was sticking up. "Given the circum-stances, I'm not sure we want to put too much faith in that."

"No. His maps are amazing, and this one is all scribbled. But this is — ohmygosh . . ." She took the map to the window where there was more light. "It's the Catacombs. The exit is marked . . . and then there's like a path traced to someplace else!"

"Where?" Henry stretched and walked over to the window.

"Wherever this is." Anna pointed to the map. A shaky blue pen line went from a star marked *Catacombes Sortie* up the street, around a couple turns, and to another star with a big barbed arrow point-ing south.

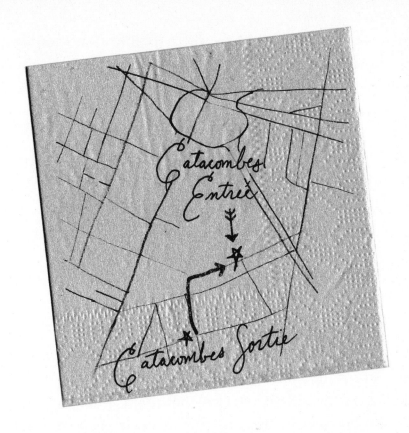

"You guys, I bet this is where they are! Our parents! This must mean . . . I bet they can't recover the painting so we have to do it and then take it to them and then . . ."

"And then we'll all live happily ever after?" Henry scoffed. "Dude, we have no clue who left this here."

"That's true," Anna admitted, studying the map. "And I don't recognize the writing. Do you, guys?"

"No," Henry blurted, but as soon as the word was out of his mouth, he realized it was wrong. "Actually,

147

wait . . ." He reached for the napkin. "That's totally how Aunt Lucinda's makes her Cs. But there's no way she'd come here to leave a map and not talk to me. Not with everything going on."

"Maybe someone else delivered it," José said.

"Who? And when?" Henry handed the napkin back to Anna and thought about waking up in the cold. Could Gilbert or someone have climbed in the window and left the map without him noticing? It was too creepy to say out loud.

"It doesn't matter," Anna said, tucking the napkin into her pocket. "We know what we need to do."

Henry had a bad feeling in his stomach, the way he felt when he got to level twenty-four on his Storm the Castle game. He knew he was going to die when the knights started shooting flaming arrows, but he always tried to run through them anyway. "Fine," he said, even though he could already hear electronic doom music in his head. "Let's go."

· • ◎ • ·

They got to the Catacombs entrance a little before eight. Nobody was around except two old ladies sitting on a bench. One had enormous sunglasses that made her look like a giant, white-haired bug. The other was rummaging through a purple fanny pack that seemed to have a whole suitcase worth of junk crammed into it.

"They open at ten. The line starts behind us." One of the old ladies said, looking at the kids over her bug-eye shades.

"No problem," Anna said, and stepped back a little, motioning for Henry and José to come closer. "It's good that we're early," she whispered. "We need to talk. I've been thinking that we need a code name for the painting. We can't be chatting about this in public using her real name."

"What do you want to call her?" Henry asked. "M.L.?"

Anna shook her head. "Too obvious."

"We could call her ... umm ..." Henry thought about the girls in his grade. "Emma? Brittany?"

"*Brittany*? That's totally undignified."

"Actually," José said thoughtfully, "it's perfect. No one will associate a modern name with a priceless work of art."

"That's a good point." Anna looked annoyed, but she nodded. "So when we find ... Brittany ... we need a way to sneak her out of the museum. Back in Boston, I heard my mom say a lot of the stolen paintings had been sliced out of their frames. If that happened to Brittany, I'm guessing the canvas will be rolled up. I brought my backpack, but the sign up there says they have the right to search bags. To make sure people don't steal bones."

"In level fourteen of my Super-Heist game, one of the guys sneaks like a hundred thousand dollars out of a bank in his pants," Henry said. "He duct-tapes the money to his legs."

"That might actually work." Anna, who was wearing a long shirt with leggings, looked at José, whose jeans were really skinny at the bottom. Then they both looked at Henry.

"No way." He tugged his baggy jeans up higher. He should have kept his mouth shut. "I can't hide the *Mona Lisa* in my pants!"

"You mean *Brittany*!" Anna whispered, nodding toward the old ladies on the bench and gesturing to the line behind them, which already had another few dozen people in it.

"Okay, *Brittany*. But I can't. That's like totally disrespectful. Aunt Lucinda would kill me."

"Henry . . ." Anna leaned in close. "If we find her, we'll be saving what may be the most famous piece of art in the world. Don't you think we should do whatever it takes?"

"Aw, man . . ." Henry wished he'd listened to his dad and gotten some school pants that weren't so droopy. "I guess. But I don't have any duct tape."

Anna frowned. "What about string or something?"

Henry checked his pockets and pulled out his SuperGamePrism charger cord. "This is all I got."

Anna nodded. "That should work."

There wasn't any more planning to do, so Henry counted people as the line grew. He watched a pigeon trying to get a crumb under the old ladies' bench. Every time it got close, the fanny pack lady would stomp her foot, and it would scurry away again.

Henry was about to go crawl down there, get the crumb, and throw it to the dumb bird when Anna grabbed his arm and pulled him behind the bench, along with José. "They're here!" She pointed to the big metal door, where the two Serpentine Prince guys from the Louvre were arguing with a Catacombs worker.

"They're trying to get in ahead of everyone," Anna whispered.

"Doesn't look like they're having much luck," José said.

The worker kept shaking his head, pointing to the back of the line, which stretched halfway around the block now. The sumo wrestler put a hand in his pocket, and for a second, Henry thought he'd pull a gun or a knife or something, but then he slipped out a pocket watch, sighed, and motioned for the skinny guy to come with him to the end of the line.

"Dude, I can't believe they didn't force their way in," Henry said. "What kind of bad guys *are* they?"

"They probably didn't want to make a scene," Anna said as the worker started unlocking the door to let people inside. "That's lucky for us, but we'll need to be fast. We have to find what we're looking for before those guys get inside." Anna paid for the tickets, and they followed the old ladies, one slow step at a time, down a spiral staircase that never seemed to end.

Henry looked up at José, descending behind him. "How far down does this go?"

José unfolded the brochure he'd grabbed at the entrance. "One hundred thirty steps. Twenty meters."

Finally, they reached the bottom, and the old ladies started shuffling their way down a narrow stone tunnel.

The one with the big sunglasses perched them on top of her head and gave a loud sniff. "Musty down here, isn't it, Bertha?"

"Excuse me," Anna said as they squeezed past the women and hurried along the passage. The air did feel heavy and damp. The ceilings were getting lower, and Henry had to duck to get through one of the doorways.

"We must be in the remains of those old quarries Hem was talking about," José said as they hurried past the interpretive signs along the empty halls. Stone pillars seemed to be holding up the ceiling. Henry hoped they were solid.

They turned, and the hallway opened up into a big room with an elaborate sculpture of a mansion carved right into one of the stone walls.

"Whoa . . ." José paused and read the panel next to it. "This says the artist was a quarry inspector. It's a model of some fortress where he fought."

Henry stared at the intricate carving. The building's tiny front steps had been carefully chiseled, one by one. "This must have taken forever. Who'd want to spend all that time down here?"

"Not me," Anna said. "Come on." They followed a shadowy hallway into another dimly lit open space. There were no stone fortresses here, but the far side of the room had a doorway with words engraved above it:

ARRÊTE! C'EST ICI L'EMPIRE DE LA MORT

"Oh, I just saw this. . . ." José flipped through his brochure. "It means 'Stop! This is the empire of death.'"

Worst. Welcome sign. Ever, Henry thought. But he followed Anna through the doorway.

And found himself facing a solid wall of bones.

He took a step forward. "This is . . . this is . . ." The pictures online had been creepy enough, but this room was overflowing with real-life, in-your-face awfulness. Even the air felt full of death. Henry could barely breathe anymore.

"There's that quote," José whispered.

On a smooth stone slab, surrounded by bones, was the poem from the napkin.

Ils furent ce que nous sommes,
Poussière, jouet du vent;

Fragiles comme des hommes.
Faibles comme le néant!

Henry remembered the translation.
They were what we are . . .
Alive, once. But now their bones were in heaps, and nobody even knew their names.

Henry looked at José, who was staring at the stone inscription. The wall of bones had even stopped Anna in her tracks. She was kneeling, staring into the eye sockets of a yellowed skull, and for once, she didn't have anything to say.

Something dripped on the back of Henry's neck, and he looked up. The ceiling was full of stubby, slimy-looking stalactites like the ones he'd seen on his class field trip to Howe Caverns in second grade. Henry wiped his neck with his hand. He didn't even want to think about what was in this water. "Come on, you guys. Let's get out of here."

"Yeah . . ." Anna said, finally breaking eye contact with the skull. She stood up, brushed off her knees and blinked a few times, fast. Henry could tell she was trying to get her brave back, but that wasn't easy down here. "We need to watch for the crossbones. Remember the photo on that lady's website?" Anna held up her pointer fingers, crossed like an *X*.

José nodded. "'The spot marked with imperfect *X*.'" And they started down the hallway of bones.

At first, Henry looked all over for the imperfect X. But it felt like the walls were getting closer, pressing against his chest. He took a deep breath — *just keep walking* — and stared straight ahead at the back of José's messy hair. But even though he tried not to look at the bones, it felt as if the bones were looking at him.

A light-colored stone cross stood out from one of the walls, shored up by bones on every side. Whoever arranged them had made patterns. A wall of leg bones, all stacked tight, with a border of skulls along the bottom and more arranged in an arch over the cross.

Henry swallowed hard. Every one of those skulls belonged to a person who used to be alive. Someone with stories and a life and a family. Maybe a baby sister like his.

José kept folding and unfolding his brochure, holding on as if it were a life raft to keep him from sinking in the heaps of bones.

"Let's go." Henry tried to make his voice sound brave, but he really wanted to get out of there. How long could these tunnels go on?

They started walking again. Every time they turned a corner, Henry hoped for a staircase back to the street. But the path never even sloped up. Every narrow hallway led to another room of awful architecture. There were pillars of bones and columns of bones and pedestals of bones. Henry looked down at the floor and took a deep breath. It felt like there wasn't enough oxygen down here . . . as if the skulls were sucking it all up.

"You guys, look!" Anna called from behind him, and Henry turned around.

He'd walked right past it — a corner of bones like all the others, but this one had the skull and cross-bones design, repeated in a neat row.

"There it is," José whispered. He pointed to the last design, half missing — just a skull above a single diagonal leg bone. "Imperfect X."

TWENTY-ONE

All three of them stood, staring at the lonely leg bone.

"Now what?" Henry said.

"Well . . . I think . . . It has to be . . ." Anna looked around. But no paintings hung on the wall of bones. "It's got to be here somewhere." She got up on her tip-toes. "There's some space between the bones and the ceiling." She looked at Henry.

"No." He shook his head. "I don't think it'd be there." He sure as heck wasn't going up to find out.

Anna rummaged through her backpack for a flashlight and handed it to José. "Hold this."

He pointed it at the top of the wall, and Anna jumped a few times. "I can't see anything."

"Did you look over here?" Henry started to turn but tripped over Anna's backpack and stumbled toward the wall. Instinctively, he raised his arms to stop himself and ended up with a handful of cool, smooth skull.

"Gahhh!!" Henry jumped back. A leg bone jabbed him in the hip and made an awful crunching sound as it slid deeper into the wall. "Geez!" Henry shook his hands as if that would get the skull germs off. He turned back to look at the wall. "They're all just . . . loose in there, not even cemented together or anything."

José stepped up to the wall, squatted down, and hesitated. He handed Anna the flashlight, then poked at one of the leg bones.

"Dude, I can't believe you're touching that on purpose." Henry shook his hands again. They still felt all clammy and dusty.

José didn't answer. He poked at another bone near the half-a-crossbones. And then another one. Finally, he found the one that Henry had pushed deeper into the wall. He worked his fingers around the bulgy part on the end and wiggled, pulling little by little, until the bone slid out from the wall and into his hand.

"You have got to be kidding me." Henry stared at the bone. It felt like alarms should be going off or ghosts should be swooping in to stick the thing back in the wall.

José turned to Anna. "Got that flashlight?"

She clicked it on, squatted down next to José, and shined the light into the space where the bone had been. Henry crouched down to look. Way back in the open space was a rolled-up something.

"That's it. That has to be her." Anna tried to shove her hand into the space, but her knuckles didn't even make it through.

"We gotta make the hole bigger." Henry looked at José. "Pull out another one."

José tried, but the next bone was stuck fast. "You're stronger. You try."

"Hurry up," Anna said. "People are coming!"

Way off in the distance, from one of those long stone-bone hallways, Henry heard voices. He took a deep breath, reached for the bone, and tried to move it. It didn't budge.

"Give it some muscle, will you?" Anna looked ready to punch him.

"I'm trying!" Henry glared at her. "But it feels wrong to be yanking somebody's bones around."

"Just do it! I'm sure whoever that was will understand!"

Henry took a deep breath. He could hear the voices — quiet but getting closer for sure — and he knew the Serpentine Prince guys were somewhere back in that line. They had to get the painting while they had the chance. So Henry got a firm grip on the end of the bone and tugged. It made a tired scraping sound and moved a tiny bit.

"Pull harder!" Anna looked anxiously down the dark hallway.

Henry wiped his sweaty palms on his pants, braced his legs against the bottom of the wall, and grabbed the bone again. He pulled with all his weight and felt it start to move. Just a tiny, begrudging little bit — and then he went flying.

"Oww!"

"Shhhh!" Anna hissed, and plunged her arm into the dark space Henry had opened up. Slowly, she pulled a long, rolled-up tube of old canvas out of the crevice.

"Is that it?" José whispered. "We better make sure."

With shaky hands, Anna unrolled the canvas. It cracked in complaint, but they saw what they needed to see — a dark wood color at the bottom of the weathered canvas, and then the yellowish-fleshy-beige of the *Mona Lisa*'s quiet hands.

"It's her. It's Brittany." Anna stared.

"Roll it back up," José whispered, and then motioned to Henry. "Pull up your pant leg and give me that cord. People are coming!"

"Oh." Henry had forgotten that Brittany was leaving with him. He handed José the GamePrism cord and pulled up his pant leg.

José knelt down and looked up at Anna. "Hold this and I'll tie, okay?"

She knelt down, too, and Henry felt the cold, scratchy length of the canvas against his calf and the inside of his knee. It tickled.

"Hold still!" José hissed.

"I can't help it!"

José wound the cord around the rolled-up painting and Henry's leg.

"You gotta make it tighter." Henry could already feel it moving.

"The cord's too slippery," José said. "And there's nowhere to put this plug."

Henry tucked the plug into his sock and took a step. The painting slipped. "This isn't gonna work."

The voices down the hallway were getting louder.

"I wish we had rubber bands or — oh!" Anna reached back and yanked out the elastic thingy that was holding her ponytail. Her hair flopped onto her shoulders. "Henry, come back!"

He pulled up his pant leg and held up his foot so Anna could wiggle the ponytail thing over his sneaker. She pulled the elastic wide, over the painting, holding it tight to Henry's calf. "There. That's better."

"Easy for you to say." Henry pulled his pant leg down just as the two old ladies walked into the room. They looked at Henry, Anna, and José, then down at the two bones on the floor.

"Isn't that awful?" Anna made her eyes all big. "Somebody must have vandalized it."

The ladies looked suspiciously at Henry and José before they continued down the hallway. "You know, after a while," one said, "all these bones start to look alike."

Henry, Anna, and José followed them. Henry hoped they were close to the exit. He couldn't really bend his knee, and Anna's ponytail thing was cutting off his circulation.

Halfway down the hall, the old ladies stopped to read another informational plaque, and Anna motioned for Henry to pass them. "We need to get out of here," she whispered. "Those Serpentine Prince guys might be in by now."

The painting scratched the inside of Henry's ankle every time he took a step, but finally, they made it down the last dark hallway to a spiral staircase.

Henry had to climb every new step with his left leg — the one with no Brittany strapped to it — and then drag his stiff painting leg up to meet it.

"You're doing great, Henry." José looked down at his brochure. "Only seventy-nine steps to go."

Finally, they climbed up into the sunlight. One of the worker guys at the top looked down at Henry's leg and said something in French.

"What?" Henry tried to look innocent.

The other guy spoke English. "He asks if you have been hurt." He nodded at Henry's leg. "You have somewhat of a limp."

"Oh!" Henry's whole body flooded with relief. "That's nothing. I . . . uh . . . hurt my knee a while ago playing football, so I have a tough time with stairs."

"Oh." He said something in French to the other guy, who nodded and looked relieved that Henry's injury wasn't his problem. "Have a good day."

They walked halfway down the block before Anna pulled the yellow napkin map from her pocket. "We have to turn left down here, and then right, and then we'll be there!"

"Only we still don't know where *there* is," José said.

"We'll find out soon!" Anna practically skipped down the sidewalk, and Henry hobbled as fast as he could to keep up. He hoped she was right — that they were about to meet up with their parents and Aunt Lucinda at some other safe house, and then Henry could give up the painting and get the feeling back in his leg, and everything would be great.

But he couldn't help thinking about Shadow Rogue Assassin and the trap that Maldisio set in level ten. His fake treasure map led right into an alley full of swordsmen.

"Here we are!" Anna stood in the middle of the sidewalk, looking around. They were right where they were supposed to be, right where the star was on the map. Way down across the street, on the other block, there were some shops and what looked like a warehouse with wooden crates stacked outside. But the only building nearby was a tiny Laundromat.

"Maybe there's a society meeting place in its basement," José said, "like that pizza place in Boston."

They went inside. It was empty except for a young couple smooching in the corner while their clothes went around and around in a dryer next to them.

Anna cleared her throat. *"Excusez-moi,"* she said, and the couple turned around. *"Avez-vous* . . . um . . . do you speak English?"

"Un petit peu." The woman held up two fingers very close together in the international symbol for *a very tiny bit.*

"Have you seen our parents? Or, like, anybody?"

The woman shook her head.

"Is there another room here? Like downstairs?"

"C'est tout," the man said, gesturing around the room. *"Au revoir!"* He waved and turned back to the lady.

"Either they're really good at being undercover," Henry said as they headed back outside, "or that map is totally bogus."

"But it's your aunt's handwriting," Anna argued. "And it says we're in the right place. Right here!" She pointed down, and Henry noticed a round metal circle under her feet.

"Let me see that map." He took the napkin and stared at the star. "This arrow isn't only pointing south. It's pointing *down*." He pointed to the manhole cover leading to the other Paris . . . the one where Hem said it was so easy to disappear.

"Ohmygosh!" Anna jumped off the circle as if it might suddenly open up and suck her down who knows where. She knelt and poked at the edge. "It's all sealed."

"We need a crowbar," Henry said, "like Hem had yesterday!"

"Oh, like we're going to happen to have one of those?" Anna made a face. "There's no way our parents would send us down there. And like Hem said, it's all damp — no place for a painting. That arrow must mean something else."

"I agree. I can't imagine them directing us to enter an off-limits tunnel." José looked around. "Especially knowing we'd be unlikely to have the right tools to gain access to . . ." He trailed off and squinted at the garbage can by the Laundromat. Then he walked over to it. "Never mind what I said." He reached behind the can and pulled out a crowbar.

"Okay, that's just weird," Anna said.

"Not really." Henry took the crowbar from José and stepped up to the manhole cover. "It makes sense they'd leave it for us. We need it to follow their map." It was all making sense now. Maybe he was just happy to be aboveground again, but Henry finally felt like this might all work out. They'd find the grown-ups, deliver the painting, and then they could go home! He had that great end-of-game feeling he always got when his avatar was running toward the finish line in Treasure Quest. "Let's go!"

José looked down at the circle of rusty metal. "But it's damp down there. . . ."

"They must have found a dry tunnel or something. How else do you explain this?" Henry held up the crow bar. "Besides, the arrow was pointing *down*. We have to go." He pulled up his pant leg, tugged off the ponytail holder, unwound the cord, and handed it to Anna, along with the painting. "Put this in your backpack now, okay? And you guys keep an eye out for people." He tried to remember how Hem had positioned the crowbar to get the other cover off.

Thankfully, the street was deserted, and the smoochy couple in the Laundromat was happy to be left alone, so nobody noticed Henry grunting and pushing and prying and sweating. Not even when the manhole cover finally came loose and Henry dropped it, clanging on the sidewalk.

Anna took out her flashlight and pointed it into the hole. Henry peeked down, and his end-of-game feeling faltered a little. There were metal rungs set in the wall, but you couldn't quite call it a ladder. It looked wet down there. Slimy, too.

"Well . . ." Henry took a deep breath and looked up at Anna and José. If the Catacombs had been level twenty-four, this was twenty-five. "Who wants to go first?"

TWENTY-TWO

Henry hated Rock, Paper, Scissors. Every time he picked scissors, somebody picked rock and he got crushed. This time, he chose paper, and smarty-pants Anna had to throw out her scissor fingers and he got all snipped up, and now he was holding on to a cold, gritty metal rung for dear life.

"Can't you aim that light better?" Henry wanted to see what kind of awful gunk he was going to land in when he ran out of rungs.

"Sorry." Anna leaned down, and the light wobbled. "It's not very powerful."

Henry lowered himself down another rung and reached with his right sneaker, but this time, it didn't meet metal. He grabbed the next rung down, stretched his leg as far as he could, and felt water seeping through the toe of his sneaker. "Aw, man. It's like a lake down here."

"The water can't be that deep, Henry," José reasoned from above. "They wouldn't expect us to swim to them."

Henry reached for the next rung, lowered himself down, and felt the cool water rise almost to his knee before his foot hit something solid. He climbed down the rest of the way and found himself standing at one end of a long, flooded tunnel.

"Who's next?"

José climbed down and then Anna, with the painting sticking out of her backpack. It was too long to fit inside, and she kept stopping on every rung to make sure it was okay.

Finally, she got to the bottom and they sloshed down the tunnel. The water had a funky, thick cave smell.

Anna held her nose. "I hate it here."

"You and me both," Henry said.

"Come on." José launched into his quote voice. "You simply have to put one foot in front of the other and keep going. Put blinders on and plow right ahead."

"Who said *that*? George Washington?" Anna asked, slogging down the hallway again.

"George Lucas. The guy who made the first *Star Wars*."

"Hmph." Something dripped on Henry's head. "I bet even the garbage room on the Death Star smelled better than this."

They followed the soggy passageway to the end, where it came to a T and split off in two directions. But the meager light from the street faded fast, and Henry couldn't see either way. "Got that flashlight?" he asked Anna.

She pointed it to the left — the darkness seemed to go on forever — and then to the right, where the walls were covered with big graffiti letters that spelled something in French.

"Hey, go back." Henry pointed to the wall, and when Anna held the light steady, they saw an arrow — it had little barbs on it like the one on their map — pointing to the left. "This way." Henry led them down the long tunnel until they saw a sliver of light that looked as if it might be coming from under a doorway.

"Maybe it's them!" Anna's voice was full of hope.

The light got brighter as they approached the end of the hallway. The path was slanting now — they were going uphill — and the water got shallower and shallower until they were finally hurrying along on a perfectly dry stone floor.

"The light's coming from behind this door," Henry whispered, then tipped his ear to listen. "And there's music in there, too." Classical. That had Aunt Lucinda written all over it. Henry's heart warmed, even though his feet were wet and cold. "I think we found them!"

Anna hesitated when they reached the door. It didn't have a regular handle, but there was a steering-wheel sort of thing in the middle. "Should we knock?"

Henry rapped on the door with his knuckles. It was metal and clangy and cold. "Aunt Lucinda?"

"Mom?" Anna whispered.

"Dad?" José called.

There was no answer.

Henry put a hand on the door and gave it a push, but it didn't move.

"Try turning the wheel," José said.

Henry tried. "It's kind of stuck." He dried his clammy hands on his shirt and tried again, and this time, the wheel turned counterclockwise. There was a gritty sliding sound and a click, and when Henry pushed on the door again, it groaned open.

Henry stepped inside — into a softly lit, underground museum.

"Oh!" Anna gasped. The room was circular, like a theater. She turned around, and her face glowed in the light of dozens and dozens of candles. They rested on every rock ledge, every pillar and stair.

A wide stone bench circled the room, and half a dozen paintings rested on it, leaning against the wall.

"That's . . . that's a Monet, I think. The one Hem was talking about at the Louvre." Anna's arm trembled as she pointed to the snowy scene, flickering in the candlelight.

"You guys . . . the society must have recovered all this already," Henry said, and his heart swelled with pride. The Silver Jaguar Society was just . . . it was incredible. And they were part of it. "And now we've got the *Mona Lisa*, too."

"I am so delighted to hear you say that."

Henry wheeled around.

Hem stood grinning in the doorway — the only way out — and beside him was the man who'd chased Henry through the park.

"Now . . ." The man grinned, and his mustache twitched. "Where is she?"

TWENTY-THREE

Henry raced for the door, but the man from the park caught him in arms that felt as solid as the marble statues from the Louvre. He dragged Henry into the center of the room while Hem closed the heavy door.

"Look . . . I don't want you to panic," Hem said.

"Are you kidding?" Henry spit the words in Hem's direction, then aimed a backward kick at the man's knees. He felt a breathy grunt in his ear, and for a second, the man's stone grip loosened. Henry tried to wrench free, but he couldn't get away.

Finally, hot-faced and out of breath, he twisted his head around to catch a glimpse of the man's face. The obsidian eyes that drilled into him, the mustache, the greasy black hair . . . were all Vincent Goosen. But Goosen's skin was weathered and pockmarked.

This man's face was younger; his neck was fleshy and pink, with no trace of Goosen's signature serpent tattoo.

Henry felt hot breath on his neck. "Are you ready to listen?"

"Fine." Henry stopped struggling and, as soon as the man let him go, turned to face him. "Who *are* you?"

The man sighed. In the dim light, he looked more tired than fierce. "I am Vincent Goosen —"

"You are *not*." Henry glared at him.

"Junior." The man folded his arms and stared back.

"Oh!" Anna squeaked from the bench by the Monet, where she was huddled with José. Her eyes got huge. "You're the other son!"

One side of the man's mouth turned up. His eyes narrowed, and he let out a half laugh through his nose. "To my father, I am no son at all."

"How'd you get out of prison?" Henry asked.

Anna answered for the guy. "No, he's not *that* one. Goosen has two sons, remember? The one who got caught with him and then that other one who disappeared, like, years ago. Only . . . he's back now." She looked at the man. "Right?"

"Like magic," the man said sadly, holding out his arms as if to prove he were real.

Henry shook his head. He couldn't get over how much this second son looked like the older Vincent

Goosen. "I thought you were his doppelhanger," he whispered.

"Doppelgänger. I was going to tell you," Hem said, stepping toward them.

Henry backed up. "You set us up!"

Anna gasped. "You drew that map, didn't you? And left the poem!"

"And the crowbar." José's eyes burned into Hem.

"After I heard those guys talking at the Panthéon, it just . . . it all came together, and I knew where the painting was. But you got all weird when we stopped to get food, and then Vincent called . . . and told me you saw him in the park, talking to my mom. I knew you weren't going to listen to anything I said after that. Unless you didn't have a choice." He gestured around the closed-in room and shrugged. "So, yeah. I tricked you to get you here." He shrugged. "I did what I had to do for the cause."

Anna narrowed her eyes. "Why didn't you get the painting yourself?"

Hem laughed a little. "I got busted trying to break in there with some UX guys last summer, so I'm on a list. I can't walk into the Catacombs like a tourist anymore."

"But we can." Henry wanted to punch Hem. "So you used us. You two-faced jerk!"

"Please . . . try to understand." Vincent Goosen Junior spoke quietly. He didn't sound like the same guy who'd barked at Henry, chasing him through the park. "I am the one you should call two-faced — but it is my father and the Serpentine Princes I've betrayed. I've been in hiding, working for the Silver Jaguar Society for three years now, at great risk to myself. I know more of my father's secrets than anyone, and —"

"He's the one who led investigators to the house in Amsterdam," Hem interrupted, "where Goosen and his other kid got arrested."

"Why should we believe you?" Henry dug his hands into his pockets.

"You wouldn't, I suppose. But I am telling the truth." Vincent Junior stepped to one side, no longer blocking Henry's path to the door. "Leave if you want. We lured you here — it is true — so you would listen. But now I see the only way to prove we mean well is to let you go."

"Not yet!" Hem stepped in front of the doorway. "What about the painting?"

Vincent shook his head. "The young man is right. Why should he believe us? Look at them." He gestured toward Anna and José, still sitting on the bench, blocking Anna's backpack with their bodies. "In these few days, they have served the society more than many full members do in a lifetime, and they deserve our respect. If they choose not to believe me . . ." His eyes filled with tears as he looked up to the echoey stone ceiling. "I was not so brave or virtuous in my youth, and it is not within my rights to stand in their way if they wish to protect her on their own." He motioned for Hem to move. "Stand aside. Trust cannot be forced, only asked."

The moods on Hem's face kept changing, but finally, he moved away from the door. His eyes fell on Henry. "There. Go if you want."

Henry took a step forward, then turned to José and Anna. "Are you coming?"

José looked at Anna, then at Vincent Goosen Junior, and then back at Henry. "Vincent Goosen Senior used to be one of the good guys. If he can change sides, I'd like to think it might work the other way, too," he said. "I think we should stay and listen."

Henry shook his head, but he sat down next to Anna and José on the bench. "Fine. Tell us what's going on."

Hem and Vincent pulled rusty folding chairs from a corner, sat down opposite the bench in the flickering light, and began. "This room has been a place of resistance for many years," Vincent said, gesturing around its curved walls. "During World War Two, when the Nazis occupied Paris, members of the Resistance risked their lives, breaking curfew, stealing through the darkened streets and disappearing beneath them to meet in secret. They organized, and planned, and plotted against Hitler's soldiers from below. They were invisible adversaries, and they helped to liberate the city."

"I suppose you were there?" Henry scoffed.

"No," he answered. "But I admire them greatly."

"That Resistance stuff really happened," Anna whispered, leaning toward Henry. "We read about it in social studies."

"It is still happening," Vincent said. "Good people must take risks to counter the evil in the world."

"Look at what we've already done." Hem gestured toward the paintings along the bench. "We've recovered all but a few of the treasures from the Louvre."

"Who's 'we'?" Henry looked Hem in the eyes. "Anna's mom? José's parents? My aunt? Do they even know about him?" He pointed at Vincent. "If they're part of this, why aren't they here?"

Hem looked quickly at Vincent and shook his head.

"What?" Henry stood up. "Don't shake your head at him. You want us to believe your campfire stories? Tell us the truth."

Hem looked at Vincent again, his mouth a tight line across his face.

Vincent's face deflated. "They deserve to know."

"Know what?" Henry wanted to shove them both off their chairs. *"What?"*

"Sit down," Vincent said, wiping his brow. "And I will tell you."

Henry sat. And waited.

Vincent folded his hands beneath his chin and took a deep breath. "My father has them."

"Your father!" Anna's face twisted. "Vincent Goosen? He . . . he has my mom?" Her voice choked on the last word.

"They are unharmed, as best I know," Vincent said, rubbing his mustache with his thumb. "But he's holding them . . . how do you say it? For ransom?"

"Where?" Anna blurted.

"We don't know." Hem sighed. "Maybe somewhere in Paris. But the Serpentine Princes also have a château in Auvergne that my mum's going to check out. She left this afternoon." He nodded toward Vincent. "That's what they were talking about in the park."

Henry narrowed his eyes. "If your mom's on our side, how come the Serpentine Princes didn't get her, too? Weren't they together?"

Hem sighed. "They were. But Mum got away. She was way outnumbered and knew it was best for her to escape and try to find them later." Hem looked like he felt awful, but Henry wondered if that was real or an act. Hem was the best liar he'd ever met. "That's what she told me when she called . . . while you were running around the park."

Henry crossed his arms. Even if that was true, there were other things that didn't add up. "If they're being held for ransom, how come we didn't get a note or anything?" In Shadow Rogue Assassin, the bad guys always sent a note right away. Otherwise, how were you supposed to know how to get your kid-napped people back?

"We did." Hem sighed. "Or . . . they did." He gestured vaguely up at the ceiling. "It was delivered to a society member's town house yesterday. With this." He reached into his pocket and pulled a silver chain from his pocket.

"Mom's necklace!" Anna lunged from the bench.

Hem handed it to her, and for a few seconds, Anna stared at the polished silver jaguar dangling from the thin chain. It had been passed down through her family for generations, just like the earrings that José's mother wore. Just like Aunt Lucinda's silver jaguar charm bracelet.

A candle in the corner flickered and went out, sending up a thin line of smoke.

"So it's true." Henry had been hoping it was another lie. He looked at Vincent. "What did the note say? What do they want?"

"The *Mona Lisa*," Vincent said solemnly. "Have you hidden it? Or were you unable to —"

Anna started to turn. "We have —"

"Wait!" Henry held up a hand to her. "If you get the painting, will you give it to them?"

Vincent looked at Hem, then stood up and walked over to the smoking candle. "We'll bring it to the society." He picked up the candle, tipped it to the side, held its wick to another one, and waited until the flame brightened. He put the candle down and turned back to Henry. "They'll decide what to do. If we do turn over the painting, it will likely be lost to the world forever, and there is no guarantee —"

"You have to at least try." José's voice trembled, and he swiped his eyes with his sleeve. "If we give it to you, you'll try, right?"

"You have the painting here, then? Where is it?" Hem's eyes darted around the room.

Anna pulled her backpack into her lap and slid out the rolled-up canvas.

Hem cursed.

"I . . . I know it got a little smooshed." Anna's hands shook as she held it out to them. "We were as careful as we could be, but we had to —"

Hem cursed again and turned to Vincent. "We should have known they'd have a decoy!"

"Decoy?" Henry's leg was still sore from where the painting had scraped against it. "What do you mean?"

Vincent squeezed his eyes shut and shook his head. Finally, he opened them again. "Leonardo da Vinci did not paint the *Mona Lisa* on a canvas," he said. "He painted her on a poplar panel."

When Anna still looked bewildered, Vincent lifted his hands and outlined a rectangle in the smoky air. "Wood. She was painted on wood. And that" — he pointed to the rolled-up canvas — "is a fake."

"Then where's the real one?" Henry's head was all muddled. "And why would somebody go to all the trouble of leaving us a stupid message with a stupid riddle to find a painting that isn't even real?"

"Oh, I believe the real painting is there as well." Vincent let out a fast breath. "If it has not yet been found by someone else."

"But there was no place else they could have — oh . . ." Anna's face fell.

"What is it?" Hem looked at her.

She bit her lip. "There was a space . . . an open space between the wall and ceiling. . . ."

"That's it!" Hem looked at his watch. "It's a little past noon. You'll have a bit of queue, but you can make it back into the Catacombs before they close for the day." He stood up as if it were settled. They were going back.

Only Henry wasn't.

He turned to Anna and José. "Tell me you're not considering this."

José looked as if a whole bunch of voices were arguing inside his head. But Anna's eyes sparked. She held up her mother's silver jaguar necklace. "We have to, Henry."

"No, we don't!" His voice echoed off the stone walls, too loud. But he didn't care. "We don't have to do anything he says." He flung out an arm toward Hem. "He's been lying to us since we got here. What makes you think he's telling the truth now? Even if he is, there's no way I'm going back down there and climbing over all those bones to look for a stupid painting." The whole idea made Henry's skin crawl. "Even if we find it, how do you think we're going to get out of that place with a picture painted on a big hunk of wood? It's not gonna fit in my pants this time."

"In your pants?" Vincent's eyebrows flew up, and he looked as if he might faint. "Oh, dear Lord."

"So what do you want to do?" Anna glared at Henry. Her eyes pooled with tears, and her voice shook. "You want to leave it there? Leave our parents?"

"*My* parents aren't here!" Henry shouted. "And I never should have come here either! I'm not going back down there."

Hem turned to Anna and José, as if Henry had already left. "Will you go?"

Anna looked at José. He nodded. "If a task is once begun, never leave it till it's done." José looked up at Henry. "It's okay if you won't come. We . . . we can meet you back home after."

"Home?" Henry's voice shook. "That bookstore is not home." He practically spit the words at José. "Home is Boston. Home is where my dad is." His voice broke, and his eyes burned with tears, but it didn't matter anymore. He started for the door.

No one stopped him.

TWENTY-FOUR

By the time Henry slogged through the wet tunnel, climbed up the ladder, scrambled out the manhole cover, and trudged the mile and a half back to the bookstore, his feet were covered in blisters. He was starving, too.

"Ah, *bonjour*!" Ursa called as he walked through the door. She whispered something into her cell phone and hung up. "You are all alone?"

"Yeah." Henry's eyes fell on the sandwich and chips Ursa had on the counter next to the cash register, and his stomach growled.

"Let me guess. You did not have lunch?" Ursa laughed and handed him half the sandwich. "Where are the others?"

"With Hem." Henry couldn't even say the name without scowling.

"I see." Ursa watched Henry chew for a few seconds. "And you are not as smitten with Hem as your friend Anna, I gather?"

"You gather right." Henry still thought Hem might be lying about Vincent. For all Henry knew, the two of them had Anna and José tied up in that tunnel with the paintings by now. And it would kind of serve them right. What sort of people ditch their friends as soon as some guy with a fedora shows up acting cool? "I can't stand that guy."

Ursa's mouth turned up in a smile. "He can be full of himself, that's for sure." She ate a chip out of her bag and handed Henry the rest. "So . . . do you know where they went?"

"Back to the Catacombs."

"Back?" She tipped her head.

"Yeah." Henry hesitated. But Ursa was a society member. "We were there earlier because we found a message on the board upstairs. We thought the society members who took the *Mona Lisa* hid the painting there, and we were right, only we got the wrong one."

Ursa looked confused. "The wrong . . . one of what?"

"The wrong *Mona Lisa*. We found a rolled-up canvas, and the real one's painted on wood."

"I see," Ursa said, nodding. "And the real one wasn't there?"

"No, it is. Well . . . Hem *says* it is. But the guy's a serious liar."

Ursa nodded thoughtfully. "You realize you should have come to me with all this, yes?"

"Yeah . . ." Henry lifted the chip bag and poured the last few salty bits into his mouth. He was exhausted. But he didn't want to sleep on that dumb, hard bench. He wanted to go home and sprawl out on the blue couch in his living room and play Shadow Rogue Assassin until he fell asleep. He felt his eyes starting to get all watery and turned away, but not in time.

"Oh, my . . ." Ursa put a hand on his shoulder. "Don't worry, Henry. I'm sure your aunt will be back very soon."

That made it worse. He shook his head. "No. Vincent says they've got her and all the other parents, too."

Ursa dropped her hand. "Vincent?"

"Goosen's son. The one who disappeared. He was down in the tunnels with Hem."

Ursa's mouth dropped open in shock.

"I know, right?" Henry couldn't believe they hadn't come to Ursa for help sooner. "The guy chased me all over the park yesterday and now he's all 'Oh, I'm really on your side. I've been fighting the Serpentine Princes undercover for years, and blah blah blah.'" Henry paused. "You think there's any chance that's for real?"

"I . . . I don't know." She blinked a bunch of times, really fast, then reached for her phone by the register.

"Why don't you go up and rest a bit. I'll make some calls and get to the bottom of all this. There are plenty of people who can help."

Henry stared at the phone. "Can I call my dad first?"

She narrowed her eyes. "Why?"

"Why?" Henry heard his own voice rising again. "Because I'm stuck in this dumb city where I don't know anybody and now some guy says Vincent Goosen's holding my aunt hostage for the *Mona Lisa*. And I want to go home! That's why."

Ursa's eyes opened wide, and she pushed the phone into his hands. "I'm so sorry. Of course! Of course you must call him. I don't know what I was thinking."

Henry dialed, and the phone started ringing. He swallowed hard, and finally, his dad answered.

"Dad, it's me."

"Henry! I've been worried to death. Lucinda hasn't called since you landed. Is everything okay?"

"No." And all the frustrated, angry tears he'd blinked back — every last one — came bubbling up. Ursa patted his back until he could catch his breath, and he told his dad everything — about the awful hard benches and stupid Hem and his stupid accent. About seeing Miranda in the park with the man who turned out to be Vincent Junior. About the message and the wild-goose chases in Notre-Dame and the

Louvre and the Panthéon. And finally the Catacombs and the watery tunnel to the candlelit room full of paintings and the news. "So they've got Aunt Lucinda. Goosen has all of them," he finished. Ursa's cell phone was all slimy with tears. Henry wiped them away on his shoulder and waited for his dad to respond.

"Henry, I —" His voice broke. "I am so, so sorry. I'm getting on a plane tonight. I'll be there first thing in the morning to take you home."

TWENTY-FIVE

Henry ate pizza with Ursa, played Shadow Rogue Assassin for a while, and then got ready for bed. His dad was coming, which should have made everything better, but there was a heavy feeling in Henry's gut that he couldn't shake.

It was later, lying on his bench, staring at the ceiling, that he figured out why. When he'd finally managed to get his dad on the phone, he'd gone off about all his problems and what a big, lying jerk Hem was. He'd never asked how his dad was doing or how the baby was.

But he'd see his dad tomorrow, and he could make up for it then. He'd ask about the baby and Bethany right away. Henry yawned and closed his eyes. Some days were so long and rough that even a rotten, uncomfortable bench couldn't keep you awake.

It was late — after midnight — when Anna, José, and Hem finally came upstairs and flicked on a light. Hem went straight into the other room, but Anna and José came and sat on the edge of Henry's bench.

"Listen," Anna said. "In the morning we're going to check out —"

"I'm going home," Henry interrupted.

"What?" Anna's mouth fell open. José looked at Henry, waiting.

"I called my dad and he's coming — he's already on the plane." Saying it out loud — out loud to Anna — felt different. Like he wasn't only leaving. He was leaving her and José. But really, they were the ones who'd left him, hadn't they? Henry wasn't the one who should feel crummy. "He's taking me home."

"You're *leaving*?" Anna said it as if she were accusing him of robbing a bank.

"Yeah." Henry propped himself up on his elbows, ready for a fight, but when he saw the tired, almost-crying look on José's face, his words caught in his throat, and he remembered. Anna and José couldn't call their parents because their parents were here . . . somewhere. All they could do was stay and wait.

"When?" José asked

"In the morning."

José nodded. "So we'll be able to say good-bye then."

Anna folded her arms and glared at Henry. He

shrugged. "It's not like I'm doing any good here anyway."

"Henry, how can you say that?" Anna stood up and whirled around to face him. "Your aunt is being held captive, and you're the only society member from your family here to do anything about it and you're going to *leave*?"

Henry frowned. When she put it that way, it made him sound like a total jerk. But he wasn't. It's just that he didn't trust Hem or Vincent Junior or anybody here. Not even Anna and José, now that they followed Hem everywhere. Henry shrugged and turned away until Anna and José walked off and left him alone.

All he wanted was to go home. How was that wrong? Aunt Lucinda could take care of herself; she'd gone on a zillion Silver Jaguar Society missions on her own before Henry even knew the group existed. And Anna and José . . . well, they had Hem now. If they were so worried about Henry, they should have come with him instead of following Hem back to the Catacombs to try and find the other painting.

Henry was so glad his dad was coming, so relieved to be going home, he'd forgotten about the painting. Now, though, he wondered. He tiptoed into the next room, where José was on a bench, propped up with a pillow, reading a Harry Potter book.

"Hey," Henry whispered.

José looked up.

"I forgot to ask. Did you find it?"

"Yeah." He put his book down but kept a finger marking the page. "It was up in that space between the bones and the ceiling."

"Who went up there?"

José smiled weakly. "I was the only one skinny enough to fit." He shrugged. "It wasn't that bad. If I didn't look down, I could pretend it was just a stone wall, you know?"

Henry nodded, even though he couldn't imagine having that strong an imagination. Stones didn't have gaping black eye sockets. "Is it here?"

José shook his head. "Hem said it wouldn't be safe here, so we ended up hiding it."

"Where?" Henry wondered if José would tell him, now that he was leaving, now that he wasn't part of things anymore, but José didn't even hesitate.

"You know those street vendors with the big green booths along the river? The ones selling all the little Eiffel Towers and posters and stuff?"

Henry nodded.

"Hem put her on the bottom of a stack of fake *Mona Lisa*s, sort of hiding in plain sight. But don't tell anybody, okay? Not even other society members — Hem says it's too dangerous until they find out who's feeding information to the Serpentine Princes."

"What if somebody buys it?" Henry could imagine

some tourist packing it in his suitcase and then hanging up the *Mona Lisa* in a dentist's office in Detroit or something.

"Hem says nobody ever buys those things. It'll be safe."

"Oh, well, if Hem says so . . ." Henry rolled his eyes.

"He's not as bad as you think." José looked down at his book for a second, then back up at Henry. "But I do understand why you're leaving."

"Yeah . . . well . . ."

"I'd leave, too, if one of my parents could come get me."

Henry nodded. He couldn't wait to see his dad, but at the same time, he felt kind of awful. "Well . . . thanks." He shuffled back to his own bench and tried to settle in, but the wooden boards underneath the stupid thin cushion felt like they were poking him.

Henry reached for his SuperGamePrism and started up Shadow Rogue Assassin, and somewhere between levels twenty-seven and twenty-eight, he fell asleep, but crazy dreams made him toss and turn. First, he was running through a tunnel with skeletons chasing him. Their bones kept falling off, but they'd swoop down and pick them up again and keep running. They were catching up to Henry, calling him names. "Filthy coward! Rogue traitor!" They all spoke in British accents.

There was a drumming noise on the roof. It got louder and louder, and then a bony finger poked Henry's shoulder.

"No!" he shouted. "Leggo!"

"Henry?"

He opened his eyes and found Ursa standing there with a bakery box. The bready smell of fresh croissants mixed with the scent of old books. "I thought we might have a welcome party for your dad. I brought breakfast so you won't need to go out in this mess when he arrives." She looked toward the window, and Henry saw streams of rain pouring down the glass.

Henry sat up. "What time is it?"

"A little before nine." She smiled. "Your father just phoned. He's in a cab coming from the airport and should be here any minute. Your friends are already downstairs. There's fruit and orange juice down there, too."

"Thanks, I'll be right down." *Ursa is the best*, Henry thought. They totally should have gone to her for help earlier instead of following stupid, stuck-up Hem all over.

When Henry got downstairs, José, Anna, and Hem were huddled over the counter eating croissants. They looked up and stopped talking when he appeared in the doorway, as if they were having a secret meeting. Henry was clearly no longer part of the club.

"Don't let me interrupt you." He grabbed a couple croissants and a banana and did an about-face to head back upstairs.

"Henry, wait, will you?" Anna called after him. "I'm sorry about last night. I couldn't believe you would fly home and leave us. But it's different with our parents here. I get that, and . . ." She ran up and gave him a fast, rough hug. "We'll miss you."

Henry looked down at his sneakers. "I'll miss you guys, too. But I . . . I gotta go home."

Anna nodded.

Henry glanced over to the counter where Hem was facing the other way, talking to José. "Listen," Henry whispered. He made sure Hem couldn't see him talking, even if he turned around. "Be careful of him, okay?"

"Oh, Henry." Anna sighed. "I know you don't like him, but he's on our side. You don't still think he's one of the bad guys, do you?"

"No, but . . ." Henry couldn't shake the memory of Hem's mom talking to Vincent Goosen Junior in the park, the ferocious look on the man's face as he'd chased Henry through the trees. What if they really were on the other side? "I'm not sure Hem knows who the bad guys are. So be careful. Okay?"

"Okay." Anna turned back to the counter as a yellow taxicab pulled up outside, its windshield wipers swishing like crazy.

"Dad!" Henry ran for the door, but Ursa was already unlocking it, opening it with a big smile. Mr. Thorn climbed out of the cab wearing his blue police jacket with the white reflective stripes and carrying a small suitcase.

Henry flew out the door into the rain, ran to his father, and hugged him so hard he almost knocked him off the curb. When he finally let go, tears were streaming down his dad's face, mixing with the raindrops.

"I am so sorry I didn't come sooner. When I didn't hear from you or Lucinda after the first day, I thought it was her usual tunnel vision with the society and she'd forgotten to touch base. I've been so busy with the new baby. . . ."

That reminded Henry he didn't want to be a jerk again. "How is the baby? And how's Bethany?"

"They're hanging in there. But —" Henry's dad stopped midsentence, staring at Ursa, who stood under the awning by the door, poking at her phone. Mr. Thorn looked back at Henry and raised his eyebrows. "Who's that? Is she . . . ?"

Henry nodded. "She's okay. She's with the society. She's the one Aunt Lucinda and the other parents left in charge of us, only . . ." He shrugged and tried to sound like it was no big deal. "They thought they'd be back in a few hours."

"Come inside, won't you?" Ursa waved them toward the door, and Henry and his dad hurried into the dry warmth of the shop. Mr. Thorn said hello to everyone, and then his eyes fell on the breakfast spread.

"Help yourself!" Ursa gestured to the counter. "You must be hungry from your trip."

"That's kind of you." Mr. Thorn turned to Henry. "But I thought maybe we'd go out to breakfast before we head back to the airport."

"Oh, no!" Ursa hurried behind the counter. "I have coffee brewing, and there's plenty of food." She looked out the front window. "This weather's not fit for man or beast. And you'll never hail another cab."

Henry's dad smiled. "It does feel pretty good to be warm and dry." He reached for a croissant. "Thank you for this, Ursa."

Henry poured some orange juice and was biting into a second chocolate croissant when a green EuroTours van pulled up outside. A bunch of people climbed out and headed for the store.

Hem looked at his watch. "Shouldn't have turned the lights on so early. We don't open for another hour."

Ursa had never locked the door again, so the first man — a heavyset guy in a green rain jacket — was already stepping inside when Hem met him. "I'm sorry, but we're —"

"Allons!" the man hollered, and in the same instant, his big bear arms wrapped around Hem as if they were made of steel. The other men from the van came bursting through the door, and Henry recognized the two Serpentine Prince guys from the Louvre, but before he could cry out or say anything, the men had them surrounded.

Mr. Thorn's hand flew to his belt, where his gun would have been if he were on duty. But his gun was back in Boston, and in the split second it took him to realize it, two of the men slammed him against a bookshelf, and a bunch of old poetry books tumbled to the floor.

The skinny blond man from the Louvre pinned Anna's arms behind her back.

The sumo wrestler grabbed José around the chest so tight he lifted him off the ground.

Another man lunged for Henry, who ducked low and almost got away. He tripped over one of the small shelves by the register and books went flying everywhere. Henry stumbled through them and lunged for the door, but a tight claw closed around his elbow, and the man yanked so hard Henry thought his arm might come out of its socket.

"Dad!" Henry hollered. He looked around frantically. Ursa was the only one still free. "Ursa! Run! Get help! Call those bodyguard guys!"

"Tais-toi!" a hot voice growled in his ear, and the man dragged Henry over next to his father.

Henry turned just in time to see Ursa kiss the blond man on the cheek, whisper something in his ear, and slip out the door.

He'd trusted the wrong person.

Ursa was the traitor. And Henry had handed her everything she needed to do her job.

TWENTY-SIX

Henry's dad struggled against the two thugs holding him until one tugged his arm roughly behind his back. Henry saw his father wince. He didn't fight after that. He tried talking. "Please. . . . These are innocent children. I've only come to take my son home. We're not who you want."

The men didn't answer. They shoved Henry and the others toward the door and waited until the street was quiet, then tightened their grips and muscled them outside into the rain.

Hem caught Henry's eye, glaring as he got bullied into the van. "What else did you tell her?"

"What?" Henry sputtered. But then he understood. Ursa. Hem must have suspected her all along. That's why he told Anna and José not to say anything about where they hid the painting.

The man holding Henry grunted something in French and gave Henry a hard shove. Henry stumbled into the van's running board.

"Ow!" His shin throbbed. "I'm going, okay?" He looked over his shoulder and saw his father lean back in the pouring rain — way, way back — into the two men holding him and lift one leg in a side kick.

It caught the man holding Henry right in the side of his ribs. The man buckled and went down, and suddenly, Henry was free.

"Henry! *Run!*" his father yelled.

Henry whirled and stared at him. And froze.

His father's face twisted, and the voice that came from his mouth was like nothing Henry had ever heard before. He looked as if he might burst into flames if Henry didn't do what he said.

"Run!"

Henry leaped over the man who had been holding him. He felt fingers claw at his ankle but yanked his foot away, and then the fingers were gone and he was stumbling down the sidewalk. Henry ran as fast as he could, splashing through the puddles. Halfway down the block, he looked back, but he couldn't see his father's face. Only the back of his head as the two men shoved him into the van.

Doors slammed, and the van edged away from the curb.

Part of Henry wanted to run back to it and get in

and hold on to his dad, to go with him wherever they were being taken. Then he remembered the look on his father's face as he shouted.

Henry! Run!

His dad would never forgive him if he didn't.

So Henry ran. He darted down a narrow pedestrian street filled with falafel shops and vendors who'd pulled their scarf racks into doorways out of the rain. He splashed down an alley, and finally, out of breath and clutching a pain in his side, stumbled up to a gelato shop. Henry leaned against the wall, pressing his cheek against the cool bricks as rain poured off the awning.

The narrow street was busy, even in the pouring rain. Moms rushed along, dragging puddle-stomping kids. Men ducked under umbrellas, briefcases slung over their shoulders. And in the center of it all, Henry had never felt more alone in his life.

He was the only one left. And no place was safe now.

Where did you go when you couldn't go anywhere?

Henry didn't know, so all afternoon, he wandered in the gloom. Even when the rain slowed to a leaky drizzle, the sky stayed heavy and gray.

Henry's stomach was empty. His clothes and sneakers were drenched. And his heart was black.

All this time, he'd thought Hem was such a jerk, such a know-it-all bossing them around in his fancy-pants accent.

But Henry was the jerk. He was the one who hadn't listened, who'd told Ursa everything, who'd brought his own dad here so those thugs could grab him and wrench his arms behind his back and drag him away.

Henry was crossing the street when a car horn blasted and jolted him out of his frustrated fog. He jumped back to the curb, then looked up and saw the river in front of him. Just past the next bridge was the huge cathedral, Notre-Dame.

Henry let out a great, awful sigh. How had he walked and walked all day long and ended up here again? He couldn't go back to the bookstore, but he did have to go to the bathroom. They had restrooms at the cathedral, so he started up the street.

Now that the rain had stopped, workers were unlocking the stalls along the riverbank, opening them up to show off used books and souvenirs.

Henry stopped. Which little green junk stand had the real *Mona Lisa* buried in its stack of paintings? He hurried along until he found a stack of *Mona Lisa*s, leaning against the bottom of the booth. The young man running the stall gave Henry a quick nod. Henry leaned over and flipped through them, as if he were thinking of buying one. They all looked the same, perfect and mass-produced, and none looked even a little bit old.

But what if Henry found the *Mona Lisa* — the real one? He could turn it over in exchange for his dad, and Anna and José and their parents and Aunt Lucinda and Hem and his mom and everybody.

Henry looked up at the booth guy. "Do you have more of these?"

The man tipped his hat and laughed. "I 'ave anozzer 'undred or so in ze warehouse, but if you don't like zese . . ." He gestured to the stack. "I do not sink you will like zose either."

"Oh." Henry's shoulders sagged. He looked down at the pile of fake *Mona*s. All their smiles looked like smirks.

"Are you all right?" The man was staring at Henry.

"Yeah," Henry lied, and started walking again. He didn't see any more *Mona Lisa* paintings, but half the stalls were still closed. He'd have to come back. The weather was getting nicer, so maybe more would open up at dinnertime when the tourists were out.

Henry wandered along the river, wishing he had X-ray vision to see into those other souvenir stands. If this were a video game, he'd be able to click on them and the one with the real painting would light up or something. Sometimes, Henry hated real life.

Henry found the bathrooms near Notre-Dame and then wandered around, past a guy feeding pigeons and an old homeless lady on a bench. Finally, he headed inside the cathedral. He didn't know what else to do while he waited for the other booths to open, and this seemed like as good a place as any to hang out and think about the mess he'd made.

He had to find a way to fix it. He *had* to. He was the reason his dad was here, halfway around the world, away from Bethany and the new baby and — Dad never even finished telling him about the baby!

What was it he'd said?

They're hanging in there. But . . .

But *what*? In all the craziness, Henry hadn't asked again, and now he couldn't. His eyes burned with tears and shame. He'd screwed everything up and let everybody down. What would his mom say if she were here now?

Henry stared up at the stained-glass windows, but the bright colors only made him feel darker inside. Usually, when he thought about his mom, he hoped she could look down from wherever she was and see him, see that he and Dad were okay. But now, he really hoped she couldn't. His mom had poured her whole heart into the Silver Jaguar Society. She'd kept her promises. Henry had ditched his as soon as he decided he didn't like somebody's accent.

But maybe he could still make things right. He'd try to find the painting and take it . . . where? You couldn't exactly look up the address for Serpentine Prince headquarters online. He'd have to get a message to them somehow, without getting caught. Maybe he could find that old society guy, Gilbert. But what if he turned out to be a traitor, too? Henry didn't know who to trust anymore.

He'd have to sneak into the bookstore himself. The Serpentine Princes were obviously getting everything posted there through Ursa. Henry could leave a note telling them to meet him to trade the painting for their hostages.

But the more Henry thought about that, the more impossible it all sounded. He wandered down the aisle, looked up at the statue of Joan of Arc, and let out a bitter laugh. "Thanks a lot," he said. Saints who did such a rotten job watching over people had no business being saints.

A raspy voice close to Henry said, "She's beautiful, isn't she?"

Henry turned. It was that homeless lady from the bench. "She's not all that," Henry said.

"Oh, look more closely," the lady whispered. "She always has a message for me."

Henry was seriously creeped out, but he turned and looked because he was afraid the old lady might get mad. She looked a little crazy.

Joan of Arc's hands were pressed together, and she was staring up at the ceiling. Henry looked up, too, and the height made him dizzy, even from below. He couldn't imagine what it was like to build this place, to be way up there in the open air.

Henry looked back at Joan.

He looked back at the ceiling.

Could it be a message? Maybe he *was* supposed to do this, and up there was where he needed to be! The roof would be a perfect place to meet . . . whoever he met from the Serpentine Princes to give them the *Mona Lisa* so they'd let his dad and everybody go. Hem had talked about going up on the roof to make his maps. *You can see all of Paris from up there*, he'd said.

Henry turned to the old lady and pointed toward the ceiling. "Is there a way I can get up there? To the towers?"

She nodded, and her chins jiggled. "Out the doors and around the side of the church, to your right, you'll find the entrance."

"Thanks." Henry went outside and found a long line for the towers; it was probably like the Catacombs and you had to show up early. At least now he knew where to go.

Henry wandered back to the riverbank. More of the art stalls had opened, and at least a couple had *Mona Lisas* out front.

Henry flipped through the paintings at the first stall near the corner, but like the others, they looked identical and new. He checked two more *Mona Lisa* piles and was starting to worry again that somebody had already bought the real one when he saw one more souvenir stand with smiling ladies stacked in front. A middle-aged woman was running the shop. She reminded Henry a little of his mom, with an easy smile and black braids tied up in a colorful scarf.

"I'm . . . looking for a painting," Henry said as he lifted the top *Mona Lisa* from the stack.

"Are you now?" The woman's eyes danced, and she fingered the pendant on her necklace. Henry stared. "Is there something wrong?" the woman asked.

Henry didn't answer; he was too busy staring at the silver jaguar that dangled from the chain at her neck. José didn't tell him Hem left the painting with a society member! Would she still let him buy it?

"No. Everything's fine. I . . . uh . . ." He looked back down at the stack of paintings and carefully lifted all but the last one from the pile.

The last painting was different. It had the same smile, the same flowing dark hair, the same quiet hands, but deeper eyes and an older finish. The paint near her elbow was a little irregular, a little bit off. Henry looked up at the woman in the scarf. "I'd like to buy this one." He held his breath waiting for her response.

She looked at Henry for a few seconds. "They sent you?"

He nodded. He had to let her think he was here for the society.

"One moment," the woman said loudly. "I need to help another customer." And she nodded to an older man who had sauntered up to the rows of little Eiffel Towers. She glanced back at Henry. "That reproduction you were looking at is a bit damaged. You may have it at no charge. But be on your way. I'm busy."

Henry nodded, then looked down at the painting. He reached out for it and hesitated, imagining the zillions of alarms that would have gone off if someone even thought about getting too close to it at the Louvre. But he wasn't there, and the painting wasn't on a wall, shielded by bulletproof glass. It was here on the sidewalk, and delivering it to the Serpentine Princes was the only way to get his father and everybody back.

Henry reached down and lifted the painting. It was lighter than he thought. He looked up the street. Where would he go? Where could he hide it while he made arrangements to meet someone? And how was he going to pull that off? He should have thought this through better.

Henry looked back at the woman. "I . . . need to do something right now. Can I pick this up in the morning?"

She nodded. "I'll be here by eight."

Henry eased the painting back onto the sidewalk and carefully rested the reproductions on top. Then he stood up. "Do you have a piece of paper and a pen?"

She reached under the counter and pulled out a huge black sack, with a sparkly, beaded Eiffel Tower on the front. It reminded Henry of their first day here, when Hem promised to show them the real tower, sparkling at night. How could everything have turned into such an awful mess so fast?

The woman found Henry a small pad of paper and a pen, hesitated a moment, then reached into her sack again and pulled out a paper bag with a baguette sticking out the top. "Here. There's water and a bar of chocolate in there as well."

Henry's stomach rumbled. "Thanks. You don't by any chance have a Band-Aid, too, do you?"

She did. "Here . . ." She handed him a handful. "Take extras. You never know."

"Thank you." Henry shoved them in his pocket, took a deep breath, and headed up the riverbank toward the bookstore.

TWENTY-SEVEN

The sun came out in time to cast long afternoon shadows and dry up the last puddles on the sidewalks. Henry crouched behind a low stone wall across the street from the bookstore and wolfed down the baguette. He took a tiny bite of the chocolate — he wanted to make it last — and started working on his message.

Dear Serpentine Princes,

Henry was pretty sure you put a comma after the greeting. But that was in a friendly letter, and this wasn't really a friendly kind of thing. Maybe he should write a business letter. But he couldn't remember what Mr. Sharp had said to use for punctuation after the greeting. A colon?

Henry peeked over the wall at the bookstore. He

could see the shapes of some people moving around behind the glass but not clearly enough to tell who they were.

He looked back at his paper and decided that *dear* sounded too wimpy.

To whom it may concern:

That was better.

To whom it may concern:
I have the Mona Lisa.

No. He couldn't come right out and say that. And he couldn't call her Brittany because Brittany was the fake, rolled-up doppelgänger painting, and the Serpentine Princes hadn't been around for that conversation, so they'd have no idea what he meant. He turned to a new page in the notepad.

To whom it may concern:
I have the lady you seek and will exchange her for those you hold. Meet me on the right tower of Notre-Dame at 11 A.M. I will be the one in the green sweatshirt.

Henry looked down at his sweatshirt. It was damp from the rain, but it was all he had with him, and he doubted he'd have time to grab clothes when he sneaked back into the bookstore.

Henry folded the note in half, tucked it into his back pocket with the Band-Aids, and looked up to the towers of Notre-Dame. The roof was crowded with tourists; Henry could see them shuffling along in line like ants. He imagined climbing up there with the painting, waiting for one of the Serpentine Princes to show up with Anna and José and Hem and the grown-ups.

Henry couldn't quite picture it. But even if the Serpentine Princes were jerks who didn't keep their part of the deal — even if they didn't bring their hostages and let them go — Henry would be up high enough to see where they were taking the painting. And then . . . well, then he'd have to figure out something else.

A car horn honked, and Henry jumped up to look over the wall. Ursa was crossing the street against the light, walking away in a hurry.

Henry wanted to follow her, but he knew this might be his only chance. He climbed over the wall and crossed the street to the bookstore.

Peering in through the window, he could see a bunch of senior citizens milling around the cash register waiting to check out. And with Ursa gone, there was only poor old Gilbert, overwhelmed at the counter. He never even looked up when Henry opened the door and sauntered inside.

Henry's heart thumped in his chest as he moved through the stacks and shelves of books and raced up the staircase at the back of the store.

Before he went to the bulletin board, he hurried to the front room and stole a look out the window. The sidewalks were buzzing with people, but Ursa was nowhere to be found.

Henry ran back to his rotten, stiff-as-a-board bench and almost cried knowing he couldn't sleep on it tonight. He didn't know where he'd go, but he couldn't worry about that until he took care of the message.

He pulled the note from his pocket, Band-Aid-taped it to the board, and stepped back to look. It didn't stand out like the colorful napkins, but Ursa or anybody else looking for new messages would find it for sure.

Henry grabbed his SuperGamePrism from beside the bench, thankful he'd charged it the night before. But then he remembered why he'd plugged it in — so he'd be able to play NBA BreakAway with his dad on the flight home. Now that might never happen, because of him.

Before Henry left, he looked out the window over the street once more — still no sign of Ursa — and hurried into the room where José had been sleeping. His fat quote book was open on his bench. Henry picked it up and started flipping pages. He needed some of that courage José seemed to get out of the book, some of that hope.

Hope.

He turned to the *H* quotes and put his finger on a random line:

Walk on with hope in your heart, and you'll never walk alone. — from Carousel

Somehow, even though it was only words on a page, it helped. Henry thought about tearing out the page to take it with him, but he knew José would flip, so instead, he took the whole book.

It wasn't stealing. The book belonged to José — not the store — and Henry was pretty sure José would want him to have all the help he could get right about now. He hurried into Anna's room and found her backpack so he'd be able to carry stuff, and on his way out, he saw one of Hem's hand-drawn maps, rolled up under his bed. Henry took that, too. He'd give it all back if he ever saw those guys again.

No, not *if*. He'd return their stuff *when* he saw them again.

Henry slung the backpack over his shoulder and headed for the stairs. He took one last look at his note up on the board.

Please, he thought. *Let this work.*

TWENTY-EIGHT

When the sun went down, Henry learned it was hard to walk with hope in your heart when you were cold and didn't have anyplace to stay. It was also tough to get any rest because you had to spend all your time solving problems. Where to go to the bathroom. Where to find food. You had to be pretty smart to be homeless.

Henry had wandered around Notre-Dame for a while until he spotted that old homeless lady who liked Joan of Arc. He stayed back and watched her. When the cathedral shut down for the night and the square started to empty out, she headed for a side street, and so did a bunch of other people who looked like they might not have apartments.

Henry followed them to the back of a café-bakery place, and a few minutes later, a bald man came out with two boxes of bread and set them carefully next to the Dumpster. When he went inside, the people all hurried to get some. Henry hung back, but the old woman looked right at him, as if she'd known he was there all along. She motioned him over, and a skinny man with red blotches on his face handed Henry a loaf.

"Thanks." Henry ate the bread and wandered until he found a little patch of green near the cathedral. Some rough-looking guys were sprawled on benches with overstuffed garbage bags at their feet. One was sleeping. Two were drinking out of beat-up water bottles. One was talking to himself. None of them looked eager to share their benches, so Henry found a gap in the flower bed near a stone wall and plopped down in the mulch.

The Notre-Dame tower tours started at ten, but he'd go earlier, right after he picked up the painting at eight. If there was a line, he'd be in front, so he could go up and find a good spot to wait for . . . whoever came.

What if no one did?

Henry hadn't put a date on that note. If nobody found it and came in the morning, he'd have to be on the cathedral roof the next morning. And the next morning after that.

Cold wetness seeped through Henry's jeans and right up into his heart. Really, the odds of the right person seeing that message and actually doing what Henry wanted them to do were . . . He didn't even want to think about it. When he did, his throat got all lumpy and tight, and his eyes burned, and he couldn't cry. Not now. Not here, trying to sleep in a park with a bunch of guys who looked like they could knock his head off.

"Ay!" The guy who'd been talking to himself stood in front of Henry, arms crossed, muscles flexed.

"Yeah?" Henry braced himself for whatever punishment got heaped on people who slept in other people's parks.

"*Voici une couverture.*" The guy unfolded his arms and dropped a threadbare wool blanket at Henry's feet.

Henry stared at it. "*Merci.*" He was pretty sure that's how Anna thanked people in French.

The guy nodded and went back to his bench.

Walk on with hope in your heart, and you'll never walk alone, Henry thought. Maybe he just had to keep hoping.

Henry sat for a long time, staring at the church towers all lit up, stretching into the sky. He wondered if their candle was still burning inside. He hoped Joan of Arc would try a little harder this time.

Shivering in his blanket, Henry fired up his GamePrism, rounded up some cartoon bad guys, and dozed. All night long, he woke and startled, then remembered where he was and the impossible job that awaited him in the morning. He couldn't imagine making it though another night like this, without anyplace to go, without his friends, without his dad.

Finally, Henry opened his eyes to sunlight. He sat up, stretched out his legs, and looked at his watch.

Seven thirty. Perfect.

Henry slung Anna's backpack over his shoulder, stood up, and shook out the blanket. He found its owner sleeping on the bench, spread the blanket over the guy's legs, and then headed for the souvenir stand.

All night, Henry had dreamed about what it would be like if this plan actually worked out. If the Serpentine Princes found his note and met him on the roof, he'd be there with the painting, ready to keep his end of the deal. And hopefully they'd keep theirs. Wasn't there some kind of code of honor, even among bad guys? In Shadow Rogue Assassin, even Maldisio released hostages when he promised.

"Bonjour!" the woman at the souvenir stand called as she removed the lock and rolled up the rattling door. She ran her hand over a row of baby Eiffel Towers, glancing up and down the street. Then she bent low and pulled a stack of *Mona Lisa*s from under the counter. "You were interested in one of these, yes?"

"Yes." Henry's heart felt all wobbly with hope. Things were actually, finally going his way. He'd survived his night in the park. The souvenir stand was open on time. And the painting . . .

There she was, smiling out from the bottom of the pile. "Thanks." Henry stood up with the painting and decided he probably shouldn't walk down the street with her out in the open. "Do you have a bag?"

The woman reached under the counter and pulled out a roll of white garbage bags. She tore one off, shook it open, and held it while Henry eased the painting inside. "Whatever your mission is, I wish you luck," she whispered, and waved Henry away.

He started down the sidewalk toward Notre-Dame but looked back at the woman once. She was watching him, and Henry couldn't help thinking how angry she would be if she knew the truth — that he wasn't going to protect the *Mona Lisa* at all, that he was on his way to climb a cathedral tower with her, so he could hand her over to the Serpentine Princes.

But he had to give them the painting or he'd never see his dad again. How could he *not* hand it over? Besides, it wasn't Henry who had promised to protect the world's artifacts; it was his dumb ancestors. Still, guilt gnawed at his stomach.

When Henry got back to Notre-Dame, he peeked into the garbage bag. "You ready?"

He was way early, but there was already a line forming for the entrance to the towers. Those two old ladies from the Catacombs were first.

"Well, if it isn't you again!" the one with the big bug-eye sunglasses exclaimed, nodding at Henry. "Where are your little friends?"

Henry's face fell. Part of him wanted to blurt out the truth — *locked up somewhere with a bunch of thugs, thanks to me* — but he blinked fast and said, "They don't like heights."

Henry carefully leaned the painting against the wall, then stood in front of it. He wished he hadn't wiped out his video game batteries last night. But on the list of things Henry regretted lately, that was kind of a small one. He pulled José's book out of his backpack to look for another quote that might inspire him. But he landed in the *D* section, so everything was about death and despair.

By ten o'clock, the line had grown to the end of the block. Henry's stomach churned. What if the Serpentine Princes found him before he got to the roof? They could totally grab him and run off. He took off his green sweatshirt and put it in the bag with the painting so he'd be harder to recognize until it was time.

Finally, a man near the door called out, "All right, we can take the first twenty in line." He unhooked a velvet rope thing, and the old ladies hurried inside.

Henry followed them up a narrow, twisty stairway that obviously wasn't designed for kids lugging bags of art and backpacks full of ten-pound quote books, so it wasn't long before he was breathing hard. Thankfully, the old ladies weren't in great shape either. The one with the fanny pack looked like her overloaded bag might topple her right down the stairs.

"Do you want to go ahead?" she asked, resting on a little landing by a window.

"Oh, no . . . you came early to be first in line. That wouldn't be right." Henry peered out the tiny window and guessed he was maybe halfway. He hadn't planned on it being so tough to get up here. He'd figured the Serpentine Princes would bring his dad and Anna and José and everybody up to the tower for the exchange, but that was hard to imagine now.

Henry started climbing again. It was like some sick joke, how every staircase in this stupid city was really like twenty times longer than it looked. The old Paris architects must have laughed their heads off, imagining all these tourists climbing and climbing. "We're almost there . . . no . . . really this time . . ." Henry was wondering if the steps would ever end when light came streaming in and the last step opened up onto the roof.

"Come forward, please, so everyone can move out of the stairway," the guide said. Henry shuffled ahead and tried to keep the painting close to him so nobody would bump it. When he looked up, he understood what Hem meant about seeing "all of Paris" from the rooftop of Notre-Dame.

This roof had a low stone wall that came to Henry's belt loops, and above that, it was caged in with wire fencing. Henry guessed that was so people didn't get ideas about climbing out to see the gargoyles, which were even cooler up close.

One looked like a troll with wings. It sat on the edge of the roof, leaning on its elbows with its chin resting on its hands, looking bored to death. Henry supposed even this great view got old after a couple hundred years. Another one — half bird, half dragon — perched on the wall looking over all the tiny people below in the square as if it might fly down and pick one off for lunch.

Henry wandered along the ledge. While everyone else was snapping pictures, he searched for a place to hide with the painting until it was time.

"All right, everyone, if you'll file this way, we'll have a look at Emmanuel, the great bourdon bell in the tower." The guide started toward a doorway.

Henry wiggled through the crowd, ducked behind a pillar, and pulled his green sweatshirt back over his head. Then there was nothing to do but wait.

· • ◉ • ·

Henry leaned against the cool stone column, watching tour groups come and go. Every time a new crowd came through, he scanned the mob for familiar faces. But it was always the same — tourists from Italy and

Japan and Texas, sporting cameras and sensible stair-climbing shoes. Henry kept waiting for the sumo wrestler or Ursa's stupid blond boyfriend, or anybody with a serpent tattoo. He watched for someone ignoring the gargoyles and way-up-high view, someone searching faces like he was, looking for an enemy to make a deal.

By eleven thirty, Henry's stomach felt hollow and growly. His back ached, his knees creaked, and he was shivering. Even sheltered by the pillar, the wind kept rattling his garbage bag. And now it was starting to rain.

Henry squatted down and retied the handles of the *Mona Lisa*'s bag to make sure no water could get in. He hadn't thought about how long he'd have to wait up here if no one came at eleven. If somebody found the note later today — say, two or three o'clock — would they come up right away or wait until tomorrow? Now that he thought about it, his note was way too vague and totally confusing. He should have listened better when Mr. Sharp was talking about clarity and specific language in writing. He should have written the date — or even the day of the week — and a range of times. He should have said he'd be there between eleven and noon, and if someone got the message after that time, they could show up the next —

"Excuse me." Henry looked up and saw a teenaged girl wearing a purple T-shirt, jeans, and bulky work boots. She had a messy ponytail and some kind of an accent, but not like Hem's, and Henry didn't think it was French either. The wind was whipping stray hairs all over her face, but when she swiped them away, Henry saw she had bright blue eyes and a wide nose, kind of like Emma, his old babysitter in Vermont.

"Yeah?" Henry stood up. He figured she'd lost her tour group or something.

But the girl nodded toward the garbage bag between Henry's feet. "I believe you and I each have something the other would like very much."

TWENTY-NINE

Henry stared at the girl. "You're the —"

"The person who has come to meet you." The girl put a finger to her lips, even though the rest of the people on the roof were way over by the gargoyles. "We got your message," she hissed, "and we agree to your exchange."

"Really?" Henry's mouth hung open. What kind of an international art-theft gang sent a teenaged girl to swap hostages for the most famous painting in the world?

"I trust you are ready to fulfill your promise?" She put her hands on her hips. Henry could see the sharp outline of the muscles in her arms and shoulders and wondered what she did to work out. Something other than playing video games, probably.

Henry's only really strong muscles were in his thumbs, so he was pretty sure she could kick his butt if she wanted.

"Well ... yeah ... but ..." Henry looked around. "Where is everybody?"

"I came alone because we imagined you would be alone. One to one. That is usually how such things are done."

"Okay. But ..." Obviously, she had more experience than Henry because he had no clue how any of this stuff "usually" happened outside of Shadow Rogue Assassin. "How am I supposed to know you let them go?" he whispered.

"I will show you." The girl turned and walked to the edge of the roof. Henry held the painting tight to his chest and followed her. The rain was picking up, running off the roof edges in streams. They squeezed between a big, drooly dragon sculpture and some killer-looking bird, and the girl pointed through the wire fence, toward a cluster of tiny people that hadn't yet raised umbrellas to shield themselves from the rain and the view from above. They were huddled around a lamppost at the far end of the square, closer to the crypt than the cathedral.

When the girl stuck her hand through the fence and waved, the tallest of the group, a guy in a long charcoal-gray trench coat, waved back from below.

"That is the head of our organization's security unit," she told Henry. "Look closely . . . I think you will recognize his companions."

Henry squinted through the rain and counted the others, and his heart raced. Aside from the tall guy, there were eight people — two short, skinny figures that looked about right to be José and Anna, one medium-size one that could be Hem, and five grown-up looking shapes that could easily be Aunt Lucinda, Anna's mom, José's parents, and Henry's dad. In fact . . . *yes*! The second-tallest man had on a dark-colored jacket with white stripes and writing on the back. That was his dad's police jacket! Henry wiped raindrops from his eyes and tried to get a better look.

But the girl's hand landed on his shoulder wheeled him around. "We must finish this business and be done." The girl's bright blue eyes darted around the roof, where only a few die-hard tourists stood holding umbrellas for one another while their friends took photographs through the rain. "You will give me the painting, and I will signal for your friends to be released. You will see our man walk away from them, but before he does, he will tell them that you are on the roof, and they will acknowledge you. Then you must wait here." The girl hadn't taken her hand from Henry's shoulder, and now he felt her grip tighten. "You will watch, and when I reach our man, we will walk away together and leave your friends to meet you below. Then — and only then — you may descend the stairs to meet them." She let go of his arm.

Henry fought the urge to rub his shoulder; her grip was seriously strong. But the girl was smiling again. "It is how we must do things. You understand, my friend?"

Henry nodded, then turned to look for his dad again. The rain was still falling in a hazy gray curtain, but through it, he could see Anna and José, huddled together near one of the grown-ups — it looked like José's mom — while the others stood hunched in the rain.

Henry turned back to the girl, held out the painting in its bag, and felt a quick stab of guilt at handing it over so willingly. But he had to do this, didn't he? For his dad. "Sorry," he whispered through the plastic.

The girl took the painting, carefully untied the top of the bag, peered inside, and quickly knotted the plastic again. She looked at Henry. "Remember. You will wait here until you see us leave," she told Henry, her blue eyes cold as gargoyle stone. "If you don't, our man has a gun under his coat and orders to use it." Her face softened. "But I know that will not be necessary. We may be on opposing sides, but we can conduct ourselves with honor." She held up the painting, and Henry saw for the first time a delicate serpent tattoo on the inside of her wrist. "I thank you for this," the girl said. Then she turned and disappeared through the doorway that led to the long winding stairs.

Henry squeezed himself between two gargoyles and stared down at the square. He waved to make sure the tall man could see him waiting like he was told. The man raised his arm, and Henry felt a little better, knowing he'd seen him. Henry wished his dad would look up, but from the sound of things, he didn't even know yet what was going on. Henry could only imagine how surprised he'd be when that girl got downstairs and told everybody they were free and Henry was up here, coming down to meet them so they could all go home.

Henry leaned forward as much as he could, until the wiry fence pressed into his forehead. He couldn't see the side door of the cathedral, but he could see people coming into the square from somewhere. He counted to a hundred, and finally — there was the girl with the painting! She carried it in front of her like a birthday cake and walked right up to the man in the long coat. Henry saw them go over to his dad and the others — then point to his tower. They all turned and looked way up.

Henry waved like crazy, jumping up and down, and when they waved back, he felt the biggest, darkest, heaviest weight in the world lift from his chest. His dad and everybody gathered around the tall man, who looked like he was passing out candy or something. Then the tall guy turned to the girl, and she looked up at Henry and waved, and both of them started hurrying away through the square.

That was it! Henry whirled around and practically flew to the doorway that led back inside. He bounded down the twisty stairs two at a time until a bunch of tourists clogged up the stairway and he had to slow down. His heart felt like it might burst out of his chest and race past everybody to rush outside on its own.

Finally, the stairs took their last twist and light filled the doorway. Henry pushed out of the crowd and raced through the rain toward the lamppost. But he wasn't even halfway there when he realized his dad — not just his dad, but *everybody* — was gone.

Henry ran to the lamppost — he was sure it was this one — the second to last — and turned in wild circles, looking for them. Where did they go? Why didn't they wait for him?

Henry's stomach dropped. What if the girl had lied? What if that guy in the long coat had forced them back to . . . to wherever they were being held as soon as Henry disappeared from his post on the roof?

"No! No!" Henry felt as if one of those gargoyles had taken a bite right out of his gut. But he couldn't give up. Even if the Serpentine Princes had taken his dad and the others captive again, they were here a few minutes ago. Right *here* — and they couldn't have gone far in the time it took Henry to race down those stairs.

He whirled around again, hoping for a glimpse of his dad or any of them — but the square was almost empty in the rain now. Even the pigeons had given up and found somewhere dry to beg for breadcrumbs.

Henry knew he didn't have much time. After the girl waved, she and that guy in the long coat had set off across the square away from the river, toward the street on the other side of the crypt.

Henry took off running that way, sneakers splashing through puddles, his face hot and wet in the rain.

When he got to the edge of the square, he looked up and down the quiet sidewalks. Up by the cathedral, there were still a few die-hard people in line for the towers, but none of them were moving. Henry turned the other way and saw a couple of people disappear around a corner. Maybe he was hoping too hard, but it looked like one of them had a dark jacket with light-colored stripes.

Henry took off again. He'd spent so much time crouched all stiff behind that pillar in the cold rain that his knees felt like they might break with every thumping step. But he kept going, pumping his arms, nearly crashing into a waiter who'd stepped out of a café door with a pitcher of water.

"Sorry!" Henry jerked to the left and stumbled off the curb. A city bus blasted its horn. Brakes squealed.

Henry leaped for the sidewalk and flailed into a café table. Silverware and plates went flying, clattering to the ground.

He weaved through the rest of the tables and turned the corner.

Yes! There it was! His dad's blue jacket with the white reflective stripes. And now Henry could read the lettering on the back. *Boston Police.* It was him!

"Dad!" Henry screamed.

His dad was halfway up the block, hurrying along with one of the moms. Henry couldn't tell if it was Anna's or José's but it didn't matter.

"Dad! I'm here!" But the roaring rain and traffic must have drowned him out. "Dad!" Henry's throat and chest were burning, but he pushed himself to run faster and finally caught up.

"Dad!" He reached out and caught the sleeve of the jacket, and the man whirled around to face him, arms raised in defense.

Henry stared.

It wasn't his father.

The man barked something in French, but Henry only shook his head. It was Dad's jacket, but it wasn't Dad. This man's face was longer, older, and marked with scars. His eyes were confused. "What you want?"

"I . . ." Henry couldn't breathe. He felt like someone had punched him in the gut, like the time he'd flown off his sled and landed on his stomach and lay there with snow creeping down his collar. There was no air here, on this street corner. Henry bent over, hands on his knees, until he felt a big hand on his shoulder and jerked back up, gasping for air.

"Who *are* you?" Henry stared at the man, tears streaming down his face. "Where did you get that jacket?"

"I trade for it," the man said defensively.

"Traded what?"

"I do a job for a pretty girl. She give me this jacket." He looked at the woman next to him — about the height of José's mom but with darker skin and shorter hair. "Her, too. And some others. We get two euro to stand in square and wave to boy on roof." His eyes flashed with recognition. "Hey! You are roof boy!"

Henry wanted to throw up. If there had been anything in his stomach, he was sure he would have. "That's my dad's jacket." It was all he could think to say.

The man shrugged. "They let me keep it."

"Did you see where that girl went?" Henry asked.

The man shook his head. The woman said something in French, and the man nodded.

"She hear girl say something about Conciergerie. Maybe they go there."

"Con-see-air-ju-ree?" Henry repeated. He whispered it to himself again. And again.

The man who was not Henry's father raised his eyebrows, then turned and started down the street with the woman who was not José's mom.

Henry watched them go, getting smaller and smaller until they were nothing but moving specks. But Henry felt even smaller than that. He'd given up the painting — his only hope of getting his father back — and watched it walk away while he stood on the roof like an idiot, waving to a bunch of stupid doppelgängers.

It seemed like the whole street was spinning. Henry could feel his heart beating in his forehead. He leaned against a brick building and slid down until he was sitting at the edge of the damp sidewalk.

We may be on opposing sides, but we can conduct ourselves with honor. He'd trusted the wrong person — again.

Now he didn't know where his dad and the others were.

He didn't even know where he was.

And he didn't have anything left to give the Serpentine Princes in exchange for the hostages.

Henry pressed the heels of his hands into his eyes — hard — and tried to push back the tears. He was done. Game over, and the end music was playing. Unless . . .

Maybe he had one life left.

Henry took a deep, shuddery breath, unzipped Anna's backpack, shoved aside José's book of quotes, pulled out the notebook and a pen, and wrote down a single word. Henry had no idea what it meant or where it was or whether it meant anything at all. But it was the only thing he had to go on if he ever wanted to see his dad again.

Con-see-air-ju-ree.

THIRTY

The woman at the souvenir stand was still there, rear-ranging her tiny monuments, when Henry came running up.

"Do you know —" He'd started to ask her about the Conciergerie, where it was and how to get there. But something made him stop. She'd want to know why he was asking. What if she followed him? What if she was a double agent somehow, like Ursa? The last time he'd reached out for help, he'd made things a million times worse. He needed to do this on his own.

"Do you know where there's a library?" he asked instead. "One where I can look something up in English?"

"I do." The woman looked at him for a few seconds. "Are you all right?"

"I will be. But I need a library. Right now. I have a map of the city. Can you help?"

He pulled Hem's map from the backpack and unfolded it, and the woman tapped her fingernail on a spot by the river. "This is where we are now. You can follow the Seine nearly all the way to the American Library in Paris," she said, tracing a path with her finger. "It's not far from the Eiffel Tower." She tapped the paper on a spot where two streets met. "Right here."

"Thank you," Henry said.

The woman searched his eyes. "Where is . . . your souvenir? Is everything all right?"

Henry looked down at the map. "It will be." It was the best he could do.

• • ◉ • •

It was after three when Henry pulled open the door to the American Library in Paris. He wandered around until he found a couple of computer workstations. They were taken by guys who looked like college students, but it wasn't long before one left and Henry slid into his spot..

He pulled out Anna's notebook and found the word. He had no clue how to spell it, so he typed "conseeairjuree" into the search engine and hoped for the best.

The screen read:

No results containing your search terms were found.
Did you mean:
Conciergerie, Conserje, Conspirare, or Consejeria

"Beats me," Henry whispered. He clicked on the first one and found a Wikipedia article. He could practically hear Mrs. Crandall, his librarian at home, hollering, "Wikipedia is not a reliable source!" But he needed quick information. It wasn't for anything official like a research paper — just to rescue a bunch of people, so Henry figured it would be okay this once.

The article said the Conciergerie was a former royal palace and prison in Paris. During the French Revolution, hundreds of prisoners had been taken from there to be executed on the guillotine.

Henry couldn't help it — his mind filled with images of his dad and Aunt Lucinda and Anna and José and their parents all lined up on guillotines with sharp blades ready to fall. He swallowed hard. What were the Serpentine Princes going to do with the Silver Jaguar Society members now that they had the *Mona Lisa*?

Henry shook his head. He couldn't think about that now. He had to find out where this place was. He scrolled down, skimming the article's subheadings until he got to "Post Revolution and present."

The article said the Conciergerie wasn't a prison or anything anymore. It was "decommissioned" — whatever that meant — in 1914, and then they made it into a tourist attraction. It said only part of the place was open to the public; the rest was courts and stuff.

Henry took a deep breath. If the place was a tourist attraction, there was still hope. He'd be able to get in this afternoon to look around. And if only parts of it were open to the public, there could be all kinds of places for the Serpentine Princes to hide his dad and the others. Henry could sneak away from the public areas and check out the back hallways, and —

"Are you finding what you need?"

Henry turned. The woman standing behind him was dressed all in black. She had purple cat-eye glasses and balanced a stack of books in her arms. She looked nothing like Mrs. Crandall, but Henry figured she must be the librarian. "I am, yeah," he said. "Only . . . is there a way I can get directions to this place?"

The woman's face lit up as if she'd been waiting her whole life to help a kid find this particular building. She put down her stack of books, and five mouse clicks and a smile later, Henry was walking out of the library with a map.

Henry looked around to get his bearings and realized he was right next to the Eiffel Tower. There was a ton of noise coming from that direction. If Anna were here, she'd already have her notebook out, but since she wasn't, Henry felt a weird responsibility to check things out for her. He turned a corner and found himself facing a wide-open area with the Eiffel Tower in the center. It looked exactly like the souvenir stand models.

A crowd of people carrying signs and posters clogged the park. Henry saw somebody rushing by with a sign in English: GREEN LAWS = CLEAN LAWS. "Hey, what's going on?"

"Demonstration," the man shouted. "We're calling for an environmental revolution! And with this crowd, it's going to happen!"

The whole green swirled with protestors and almost as many police officers. Henry wondered . . . "Hey, do you know if the police here . . . Are any of them Interpol?" He thought that was what Aunt Lucinda had called the international group working with the society in Paris.

"Probably. They've sent the whole official lot. But we won't be silenced!" The man ran off toward the tower.

Henry thought about following him, about finding some Interpol officers and bringing them to the Conciergerie to help. But what if his dad and the others weren't being held there at all? Even if they were, there wasn't time.

So Henry turned away from the Eiffel Tower and hurried down the street, toward the river, toward the bookstore and the souvenir stand, and, if his guess was right, toward the long-ago prison that held his dad and the others.

In about forty-five minutes, the riverbank started to look familiar again. Up ahead, he could see Notre-Dame, but the map said to cross the river before he got to the square with the cathedral. Henry did that, walked about a block, and found a small line waiting outside a gray stone building with arched doorways.

"Well, if it isn't our boyfriend!"

The two old ladies from the lines at Notre-Dame and the Catacombs were leaning against the fence outside the building.

Henry stepped up behind them and tried to pretend he was a tourist, too. "Aren't you a little late? You're not first in line this time."

"Don't need to be. This isn't one of the more popular attractions. Those you hit bright and early — gotta be in line one to two hours before opening." The woman with the giant sunglasses tapped her watch and nodded knowingly. "It's all about timing and strategy."

Timing and strategy, Henry thought as the line shuffled forward. He'd check this place out, and if he found them, he could work out a strategy for the right time and come back to stage a rescue. He'd done it a zillion times in video games. There was the castle-storming in Shadow Rogue Assassin, where he'd collected golden keys all over the castle and then used them to unlock the door to the duke's cell. There was the forest-cave rescue in Robin Hood: Mission Payback, but this place probably didn't have a dirt floor to tunnel through. The level twenty-seven strategy from his Super-Heist game was the all-time best, when the robbers escaped from the bank by blasting through the back wall with dynamite.

Henry wished he had dynamite. All he had was a flimsy map, a quote book, a notebook, and a Super GamePrism with dead batteries. But when the line moved, Henry followed the old ladies inside and grabbed a brochure that showed how the place was laid out.

The big room inside the door was all looming arches and high ceilings, more palace than prison. Henry's map took him through that open space, through a gift shop that sold little model guillotines, and into a dark hallway with iron-barred cells on one side. When Henry's eyes adjusted to the dark, he saw a man sitting at a desk in one of the cells. But it was only a realistic-looking statue.

The fanny pack lady stepped up next to him. "Gives you quite a chill, doesn't it?"

"Yeah," Henry said weakly. He was about to turn down the hallway, when a different voice spoke behind him.

". . . move them if we're going to."

Henry snuck a glance over his shoulder.

It was her. The girl from the cathedral roof. The girl who had walked away with the *Mona Lisa*.

"Why would the boy believe they are here?" a deeper, huskier voice whispered in an accent like Hem's. "I don't see how —"

"You do not understand," the girl interrupted. "The boy has no idea we dressed a beggar in his father's jacket. He believes he saw his father — and then his father was gone. What if he saw us come this way and brings help?"

"What if he does?" the man's voice hissed. "The police will come and they will find a well-run tourist attraction. Nothing more."

Henry pulled a spare Band-Aid from his pocket and dropped it to the floor so he would have a reason to bend down. He needed to be invisible. He had to hear more.

But the voices faded, and when Henry looked back, he saw only the girl's swinging ponytail as she followed the man through a doorway.

Henry stood and crept after them. He tried to keep some tourists in between, but they all kept stopping to look at things — a wall inscribed with names of guillotine victims, a display of eighteenth-century swords, a glass case full of old metal keys.

Finally, they moved on to a small, darkish room with a bed and desk. A sign said it was the cell of Marie

Antoinette. Henry looked around. The girl from the cathedral roof stood in a corner, huddled in conversation with the man. Neither was paying the slightest bit of attention to the exhibit or the visitors pouring into the room now. A tour bus must have unloaded or something.

"Excusez-moi." Somebody bumped into Henry, nudging him deeper into the room until he found himself right behind the girl from the roof. She was facing the other way, so Henry could look right at the man she was talking to. He was short, stocky, and muscular, with a shiny bald head. Henry didn't recognize the guy, and that was good. Even if the man saw him, he'd figure Henry was some kid on a field trip.

The girl from the roof shifted her weight, and Henry froze. If she turned around, he'd be right there in her face, and she'd recognize him for sure. She pulled a hand from her jacket pocket, waving it around as she spoke. Henry heard a jingle. It was too loud to be just a few coins. She had keys in that pocket.

The girl wasn't very old, but the Serpentine Princes must have trusted her if they'd sent her to get the *Mona Lisa*. Could she possibly have the keys that would open the room where Henry's dad and the others were being held? Did Henry dare try to get them?

As stupid and aggravating as Hem was, Henry wished now he'd listened better while Hem was telling José and Anna how to pick pockets. There were three steps, right? Misdirection, concealment, and . . . something else. Grabbing?

Henry looked casually around the room. The misdirection was going to be easy with so many people packed in here. Henry wasn't the only one crowded up against the girl from the roof. The old lady with the fanny pack was taking pictures, and she bumped the girl's butt with her bag practically every time she turned around. The first few times, the girl had turned, but now she didn't even bother looking annoyed.

Screening was a cinch, too — it was so hot in this cell everybody was taking off jackets. Henry pulled his sweatshirt over his head, draped it on his left arm, and tucked his right hand underneath.

Henry took half a step toward the girl, leaning closer as if he were reading the interpretive sign on the railing beside her. He looked quickly at the man, but he was whispering so fiercely at the girl, waving his hands around, he didn't even seem to notice Henry existed.

And that was perfect.

The girl's jacket was loose, and her pocket sagged open. Henry's heart was thumping out of control, but he steadied his hand and positioned it near the girl's gaping pocket. Then he stumbled into her as if somebody had shoved him, and at the same time, his hand darted into the pocket and snatched the keys like a snake striking at a mouse.

"'S'cusez-moi," Henry mumbled in a fake-deep voice, and he turned away so the girl couldn't see his face as he squirmed through the crowd out of Marie Antoinette's cell.

Back in the hallway, he shoved the keys into his front jeans pocket and tried to think clearly over the pounding of his heart. He had to keep moving. He had to find his dad and the others before that girl realized her keys were gone.

If only Henry had a map. Somewhere in one of these cells or secret rooms or — wait . . . he did have a map!

Henry had forgotten the brochure he grabbed at the entrance, but now he pulled it from his pocket and unfolded it. According to this, only a little of the building was actually museum. Some was still used for courtrooms and stuff. Henry figured the Serpentine Princes wouldn't have anything to do with that part. Bad guys hated court.

He focused in on the museum part of the map and saw there were actually more cells in the long hallway than he'd thought. He'd seen a couple of them — that one with the fake guy at the desk, and another with fake men sleeping on pallets of hay — but this map showed other cells that Henry hadn't noticed.

Henry headed back to that part of the museum. When he reached the hallway with the cells, it was deserted except for a family — a mom and dad with two little kids who tugged on the bars and pressed their faces to the openings as if they were prisoners, too.

At the end of the hallway, there was another set of iron bars, but Henry couldn't see into this cell. Behind the bars, a big metal door was closed tight. There wasn't even a handle to jiggle — only a small lock with a keyhole in the center.

He reached through the bars and gave the door a casual push. It didn't move.

He waited until the family left for the next room with the names of all the guillotined people and then gave the door a harder shove. "Anybody in there?" He didn't expect an answer. He wasn't even sure if somebody on the other side would be able to hear him.

But just as Henry turned away from the door to head down the hallway to the next cell, somebody answered.

The voice was quiet and hoarse. Tentative and tired-sounding. And familiar.

"Henry? Is that you?"

THIRTY-ONE

"Dad!" Henry forgot to be quiet. He flew back to the cell and pressed his ear between two bars, desperate to hear his dad's voice again.

"Shhh!"

"Sorry," Henry hissed, whispering at the lock. "Can you hear me if I talk like this? Is anybody else in there?"

"We all are," his dad's voice drifted out. "But this whole place is under their control, Henry. You can't stay. What are you even doing here?"

"I came to find you," Henry whispered. "I tried to get them to let you guys go, but . . ." Henry stopped. If his dad knew he'd given up the *Mona Lisa* because he didn't know enough not to make deals with rotten gang members . . . "Listen," he whispered. "I have keys. I might be able to —"

"Get out of here." His dad's voice was urgent and rough. "Now. Find a police officer and tell him you need to speak with someone from Interpol. Tell them it's an emergency and you can't talk with anyone else, and then when —"

"Dad, no." Henry swallowed hard. He pulled the keys from his pocket, chose one, and aimed it toward the lock, but his fingers were all sweaty and shaky. The key didn't fit. He chose another one. "I have keys. I've got to get you out. They're talking about moving you and —"

"No! I said get out of here. You're going to get caught. Now go!"

The second key didn't work either. Henry's hands were shaking, but he fumbled through until he found a different one that looked like it might fit.

It didn't.

Henry heard his dad curse softly on the other side of the door.

"I can't do what you're telling me to do. I can't." *Because this is all my fault*, Henry thought. He didn't say it aloud — but he knew it was true.

He tried a fourth key. And a fifth. No luck.

Fumbling for a sixth, he dropped the whole clanging set onto the stone floor.

Henry swooped down to grab the keys and froze, listening. His heart thudded in his ears, and then he heard voices. They were still far down a hallway.

Henry flipped through the keys until he found one that didn't feel familiar in his fingers and tried again. It didn't even go halfway into the lock. He yanked it out and found another key. *Please turn,* he thought. He'd tried almost all of them, and an awful idea was forcing itself into his head, no matter how many times he shoved it away.

None of them were going to work and he was never going to get his dad back. Ever.

Stop, Henry thought. *Calm down.* He closed his eyes and took a deep breath.

And heard footsteps.

Clunking boot steps on stone.

Henry's eyes flew open. His dad was quiet inside the cell, but Henry knew if he had any idea what was coming, he'd have screamed for Henry to go — run — get out.

Henry couldn't do that. Not without his dad. If he couldn't leave with everybody, he wasn't leaving at all. He stared at the keys in his hands. One more. He had time to try one more.

If this were a video game, the right key would sparkle or glow or something. Henry was hating real life more by the second — why did all the stupid keys have to look alike? He grabbed what he thought was the last one he hadn't tried, shoved it into the key-hole, squeezed his eyes shut, and twisted his hand to the right.

The key turned.

Yes! Henry reached through the iron bars, pressed both hands against the cold metal door, and pushed. It was heavy — heavier than the big old oak door on their apartment building in Boston — but it creaked open a little, and then Henry saw his dad's big hand wrap around the edge of the door and pull it open.

"Dad!" Henry forgot everything else. He reached through the bars and grabbed at his father.

"Henry!" His dad's voice was choked, and his face was all twisted. He squeezed Henry's hand once — hard — and then pushed it away. "Get out of here! Go do what I said!"

"But I . . ." Henry was about to say he'd unlocked the door — but the solid bars pressing into his chest were like a hard, cold laugh in his face. Henry stared through them at his dad, Aunt Lucinda and Hem, Anna and José and their parents, all trapped inside. "I . . . I'm not going. We have to get you guys out."

He grabbed the keys and yanked them from the lock, then paused and listened hard. Muffled tourist sounds drifted in from the other rooms — oohs and aahs and shuffling steps and camera clicks — but no more footsteps. Maybe they'd left. There was still time.

But there was no neat, round modern lock on the iron bars. The only keyhole Henry could find was big enough to put his finger inside, and none of these little modern keys were going to work. It was like bringing a toy lightsaber to a medieval sword fight. He needed —

"Wait here!" Henry tore down the hallway, realizing as he went what a stupid thing that was to say to a bunch of people locked in a cell. He turned and hoped he was remembering the room with — *there!*

He raced to the glass case full of old metal keys. There had to be two dozen rusty old keys in here — some with bars for handles, others with round holes you could put a finger through. Some had curved shapes on the end that got stuck in the lock, and a few had angled metal pieces with so many turns they looked like mazes or puzzles. Panting so hard his breath steamed the glass, Henry forced himself to picture that lock. Which key would fit?

One of them in the center the case seemed to give off a glint of light. It must have been a reflection from the ceiling light, but it caught Henry's attention. It looked like the old-fashioned key that Mad Ben the Pirate used to open the chest in Treasure Quest. And it looked like it might fit the lock for the metal bars.

Just in case the universe had decided to cut him a break, Henry tried to lift the lid on the case. But the universe was in no such mood. It was locked.

Henry pulled the girl's key ring from his pocket and tried the first key, which didn't fit at all — and then another one that went all the way in but didn't even think about turning. He was looking for a good third choice when the footsteps started again, and the keys felt like ice in Henry's hands.

They were close this time — too close — maybe even already heading down the long hallway with the cells.

He'd have to break the case and hope his first guess about the keys was right. Henry looked around the room for a baseball bat — they always seemed to be in the corner when you needed one in a video game — but there wasn't even a single lousy stick in this place. There was a fire extinguisher on the wall. Henry tugged on that, but it didn't budge.

He held his breath and tried to listen over his crazy thudding heart. The footsteps were definitely in the hallway now.

Henry ran into the next room and wanted to scream. Why did these people have to lock every single stupid thing in cases? It's not like it would kill them to leave one sword out where you could use it to break some glass. His only hope was an old wooden ladder on the wall. It was all chipped and half rotting, and Henry hoped it was junky enough to be just hanging on a nail.

He tugged on a lower rung, and the bottom of the ladder lifted right off the wall. Henry crouched down and pushed up until the whole thing came free, teetering all over the place as he lugged it back to the glass case.

Henry stood as still as he could, balancing the ladder and trying to catch his breath. He listened hard but couldn't hear anyone nearby. Even the tourists had disappeared. But that would change when the glass shattered. Everybody would hear. Everybody would come running. He'd have to run faster.

He lifted the ladder high over the case, took a deep breath, and let it fall. The glass exploded into a million shards with a crash that left Henry's ears ringing.

A sharp voice echoed off the stone walls. "Hey!"

Henry dropped the ladder to the floor, grabbed the key from the center of the case, and raced back to the cell.

The girl and the bald man flew down the hallway toward him, but he forced himself to focus on the lock.

Henry's hand was bleeding — he must have grabbed some glass along with the key — but he jammed it into the hole, turned it, and shoved the bars to the side with a creaky groan. "Go!" The way this scene had played out in Henry's head, he'd waited there, staying back until everyone was out, but his dad had different ideas. He pushed Henry roughly in front of him, barked, "Move!" and hustled him down the hallway.

Henry could hear a clunking mess of footsteps over his shoulder but there was no time to look back to see who was where or even if everybody made it out. Henry raced down the long hallway, through the room with the case. His feet crunched on shards of broken glass.

When they burst into the gift shop, Henry just missed crashing into a bookshelf. He swerved and knocked over a table, and a row of little toy guillotines crashed to the marble floor.

"This way!" His dad shoved him to the right — through the grand entrance area with its tall pillars and arches — and finally, into the light of day, so bright it burned Henry's dungeon-tired eyes.

Where could they go? Where would they be safe? Henry looked at his dad, but even his father seemed lost — floundering down the cobblestone street toward the bridge that crossed the river.

All the footstep sounds were lost in traffic noises now — honking cars and whooshing brakes of public buses. Henry knew it was stupid, but he slowed just enough to look back.

He wished he hadn't.

THIRTY-TWO

The girl from the cathedral and the bald man from the prison tore down the sidewalk, getting closer with every step. A whole furious mob ran behind them — the skinny blond man and the sumo wrestler from the Louvre and at least a dozen more thugs who probably had snake tattoos on every limb.

In the middle of the pack — Henry knew his face the second he saw it — was the leader of the Serpentine Princes himself, Vincent Goosen. His mouth twisted in a ferocious scowl.

"They're coming!" Henry yelled, and put on a new burst of speed. "A whole mess of them! Come on!"

He raced over the bridge and turned along the river, gulping big breaths of city air and sneaking glances over his shoulder. His dad was half a step behind him, with Anna and José and everybody right on their heels. Henry strained to see past them to Goosen and his men, but his father pointed forward.

Henry knew he was right. No sense in watching doom catch up with you. Their best hope was to keep going and hope for a miracle. But even as Henry pumped his legs, he imagined the end-of-game music getting louder. They couldn't run forever. Henry had barely slept or eaten in two days, and his dad and the others had been locked up in that awful, cold-stone place. How long could they last?

Henry stopped short — he'd almost crashed into a bicyclist — and in the instant before he took off again, he stole a quick look at his dad, whose face was sweaty and determined. Henry couldn't let his dad down now. He needed a plan. He had to get them some-place safe.

Henry looked around frantically. They could cross the other street and head away from the river toward — was that huge building the Louvre? But then what? They couldn't just barge inside, and they sure couldn't count on museum security to help — not after the Serpentine Prince infiltration that had allowed the huge heist in the first place.

So Henry kept running. He didn't know how far they'd gone or how long it had been since they burst out of the Conciergerie. He was starting to feel like this would all never end — like they'd go on running through the streets of Paris forever — when a car horn blasted. Henry felt his dad's hand close hard on his elbow and yank him back from the street.

Traffic was so thick here, so rushed and chaotic, there was no way they could cross against the light. Henry whirled around. Goosen and the girl and the rest of them were mired in a mob of tourists half a block away, but they were shoving and elbowing, fighting their way through the crowd. There wasn't time to wait for the light, and the only other option was a set of stairs that led away from the street, away from the honking, clogged-up traffic, and down to the riverbank.

"Down here!" Henry turned and raced down the steps before his dad or anyone else could question it. At the bottom of the steps, one of the Batobus tour workers was untying a boat from the dock.

Henry thought fast — they were way past the Louvre, so this had to be the next stop, which was . . . José would remember. "Hey!" he screamed over the traffic noise. "Remember that Batobus poster we saw? Where does this stop after the Louvre?"

José's face was all red and sweaty, but he didn't hesitate. "Champs-Élysées and then the Eiffel Tower!" he called.

"And there's nothing in between those two? You sure?"

"*I'm* sure," Hem answered. "But why —"

"Nevermind — just come!" Hem could follow him for once. Because the Eiffel Tower might be their only hope now. "Wait!" Henry screamed, waving like mad to the guy at the boat's control panel as it started to pull away from shore.

But the man shook his head, and a crew member closer to Henry shouted, "Sorry! Ze next boat is loading now. You can catch zat one!" He pointed to another boat down the river. A long line of tourists shuffled along, waiting to get on board.

Henry wanted to scream. If they waited for that line — he glanced up to the top of the steps and saw the girl from Notre-Dame. She pointed and then started thundering down the stairs with Goosen and the rest of them behind her.

"Come on — we can make this! Don't stop!" Henry took off like a track star at the gun, running straight for the riverbank just ahead of the moving Batobus. He tried to imagine the hope in his heart giving him a boost. He needed to make this jump. He needed his dad and the others to follow him and make it, too. And then, he needed to find what he hoped they'd find when the boat arrived at the Eiffel Tower.

It was only a dozen steps to the concrete edge of the riverbank — not far enough to get up half the speed Henry had hoped for — but his sneaker gave the pavement one last thump and then he threw himself forward, leaping for the open part of the boat's deck.

He made it by more than he'd expected and scrambled away from the edge, into the crowd of gasping families and tour groups, hoping as hard as he could.

Something knocked Henry on his side, and for a few seconds, all he could see was the boat's scratched up canopy roof. He heard his dad calling to the others, "Keep coming!"

Henry rolled over and pushed up on his elbows in time to see Aunt Lucinda leap from the riverbank, arms flailing as she jumped for the edge of the boat.

She looked like she'd make it, but her foot slipped off the edge of the boat. Henry could see her arms clutching the boat's lowest railing. His dad dove through the crowd, reached down, and heaved a huffing, puffing, dripping Aunt Lucinda over the railing onto the boat. Anna, José, and Hem stood with their mouths hanging open. All the parents rushed to Aunt Lucinda's side, and José's dad took off a jacket to wrap around her soggy shoulders.

Henry breathed a sigh of relief, but not for long.

The friendly crew member was at their side in seconds, looking a lot less friendly. "I told you zat you would have to take anozzer boat. But do you listen? No! You jump and —" He flailed his arms around in what Henry thought was a pretty good imitation of Aunt Lucinda leaping. "Ze next boat was right zere!" He pointed.

The second Batobus had already pulled away from the dock, not even two boat lengths behind them. It was packed with Serpentine Princes. Goosen was at the very front, leaning into the railing, staring at their boat with a hungry smile.

"Dad, listen," Henry said, scrambling to his father's side. "These boats go to the Eiffel Tower next. I was there earlier today and there's this protest with lots of police. There were Interpol guys, and you said —"

"We need a phone," Anna's mom interrupted. She stepped right up to the not-friendly-anymore crew member. "Is there a cell phone on this boat? Ours were taken from us, and it's an emergency."

The crew member's mouth dropped open. "Who do you sink you are, *madame*? You leap onto ze boat and —"

"Excuse me." Anna's mom pushed past the crew member and hurried up to a bunch of passengers on the bench. "Does anyone have a phone we can borrow? It's urgent."

Everyone looked at her as if she were nuts and maybe dangerous. But then Henry heard a familiar voice.

"Bertha, look who's here!" Henry turned and saw the old lady with the huge sunglasses waving from a bench.

He hurried over. "Does one of you have a cell phone we could borrow? Please?"

"Certainly." Bertha pulled a phone from her purple fanny pack and handed it to Henry. "Don't give it to the wet one. It'll short out if she drips on it."

"Thanks." He passed the phone to Anna's mom, who crouched in a corner of the deck and started dialing. Henry went back to his dad, who was trying to keep the crew member busy.

Henry's stomach was all scrunched in a knot. This was their last shot. He hoped — prayed to Joan of Arc and everybody else — that he'd find the help he was counting on when they got to the Eiffel Tower.

"How long do we have before the stop?" Anna's mom was back, phone pressed to her ear, demanding answers from the crew member as if she were his boss and not some rogue boat-jumper. She glanced down at the schedule on a brochure she'd picked up from the bench. "This says ten minutes. Is that correct? Is there any chance one of the boats might make a stop before that?"

"No, zere is not." The man's mouth was pulled together so tightly it looked like someone had stitched it. "Ze boat operates on a very strict schedule and stops only at ze official Batobus terminals." He looked at his watch. "Ze next stop is in eight and a half minutes."

"Got that?" Anna's mom said into the phone. "About eight minutes. Great." And she ended her call.

"You, *madame*, will not be going anywhere when we arrive. You have broken ze law and ze captain has called ze proper authorities. Zey will be waiting at ze Eiffel Tower."

"Thank you very much," Anna's mom said politely. "That will be absolutely perfect."

THIRTY-THREE

It was true. The Eiffel Tower sparkled at night. Every hour on the hour, just like Hem said. At least he told the truth once in a while.

In the eight minutes it took the boats to get to the next stop, the sky went from dusk to dark, and when the first boat made the turn toward the Eiffel Tower, the light show began.

"Whoa." Henry knelt on a bench between Anna and José. All three of them leaned over with their elbows on the railing, staring up at the twinkling lights on shore.

"Spectacular," José whispered.

And it was. But then Henry spotted something even better than twenty thousand carefully choreographed lightbulbs. The swirling blue lights of at least twenty police vehicles lit the area around the dock and reflected in the waters of the Seine. It was the most beautiful thing Henry had ever seen.

When the boat pulled into the dock, the grumpy crew member hurried right up to the Interpol officers waiting on shore, ready to report his unruly line jumpers. But the officers pushed past him and made a protective circle around Henry and his dad and the others.

"We have an armored van to take you to headquarters," one of the female officers said. She wore a blue Interpol jacket with small yellow stars like the others, but her collar was open, and it was impossible to miss the silver jaguar pendant gleaming at her throat.

"Goosen is here — you know that, right?" Henry started to point, but the woman put up her hand and motioned him to lower his arm.

"We know. We've been tracking him for three days, and we were closing in when you decided to raid the Conciergerie on your own." She looked at him over her glasses.

"Oh." When she put it that way, Henry felt kind of dumb, even though it had all worked out. "Well, I guess we sort of brought him to you instead."

"I guess you did." She smiled. "Well done." She gestured toward the van, pulled right up to the dock with its door wide open. Henry hesitated — he couldn't help remembering the other dark van that had swallowed up his dad and everyone back at the bookstore.

But these are the good guys, he reminded himself. *We're all safe now. It's okay.*

He climbed into the van between his dad and Aunt Lucinda and closed his eyes, listening to Anna and José whispering to their parents in the back seat, listening to Hem on the police phone with his mom. His accent was less annoying when he sounded tired and scared like everybody else.

Henry was exhausted, but he still felt sort of supercharged — like the currents of adrenaline that had carried him through this whole thing weren't quite burned out yet. His fingers tingled, but not in that awful anxious way — in a good way. Like he'd finished the last level of the best video game ever. Feeling his dad's arm around his shoulders was even better than seeing his name on a high-score list.

Henry took a deep, quiet breath and tried to relax. This time, they were really going home.

The van's engine started, and Henry opened his eyes. The woman with the jaguar pendant was driving and another Interpol agent sat in the passenger's seat, staring out the window toward the river even as the van started to move. He still looked like he was on alert, and for a second, Henry was afraid to look back, afraid he'd see something to burst the bubble now that everything was finally all right. But he couldn't keep himself from turning to the window and pressing his nose against the glass.

When he did, when his eyes adjusted to the chaotic flashing lights, he saw not only the fleet of police
cars but half a dozen Interpol boats in the river. They
surrounded a cluster of Serpentine Princes who must
have leaped from their Batobus into the Seine when
they realized they'd cruised into a trap. A spotlight
from shore lit up one of the officers as he leaned over
the railing of his boat, fishing a very angry, very soggy
Vincent Goosen from the water.

This time, Henry wasn't even a little bit sorry he'd
decided to look back. It was the best thing he'd seen
in days.

Game over.

The Silver Jaguar Society had won.

THIRTY-FOUR

There was nothing like a growly, tired-of-stale-baguettes stomach to make a guy's eyes pop open when real food finally showed up.

"Le Gruyère?" A waiter in a white shirt and black bow tie put a steaming pot of hot cheese on their table and set a big basket of bread cubes beside it.

"Oui!" Henry practically shouted, reaching for a piece of bread. By the time they'd finished answering questions at Interpol headquarters and settled in at a restaurant near the bookstore, it was almost midnight, and Henry was starving.

"Forty thousand restaurants in this city, and we end up here." Hem rolled his eyes. "Only tourists eat fondue in Paris."

Henry lifted his tiny fondue fork and flicked a piece of bread at Hem from across the table. "This tourist is getting on a plane to go home in the morning. And I'm tired of those ham-and-cheese sandwiches, even though they're pretty good."

The fondue was perfect, Henry decided. Gooey and rich and hot and filling — everything that his last two days of meals hadn't been. The grown-ups were at one end of the table, huddled over their own pot of cheese and going over society plans now that Goosen was finally behind bars. They hadn't known that Vincent Goosen Junior had been working under-cover as a double agent — only Miranda and a couple other high-ranking European members knew and were working with him. Henry thought it was kind of lame that they didn't tell everyone, but Aunt Lucinda said it was the way things had to be to keep him safe and secret. They'd meet with Miranda to learn more when she returned from Auvergne.

Anna, José, and Hem were chattering on about the Interpol headquarters, how cool their surveillance equipment was, how the Interpol agents had planned to go after Goosen and whether it would have worked, but Henry was too tired to do much more than listen and nod every once in a while. He was glad to hear that most of the art from the other museums around the world had been recovered, too.

And he really perked up when he heard Anna's mother talking about plans to get all the Louvre's sto-len art back on display — including the *Mona Lisa*.

"They found her?" Henry blurted through a mouthful of cheesy bread. He swallowed. "Is she okay and everything?"

Aunt Lucinda gave him a funny look. "Well, I certainly assume so. Why?"

"Because the last time I saw her, that girl with the mean-looking boots was running down the street with her."

Aunt Lucinda tipped her head and frowned. Henry's dad squinted, confused. And that's when Henry realized — they didn't know. He'd never told them.

His stomach dropped right down to the floor, and he wasn't hungry anymore. But he had to explain what he'd done. Maybe there was still time for the Interpol guys to track her down. Henry took a deep breath. "You know when you guys left that note at the bookstore? The riddle?"

"*You* found that?" Anna's mom looked at them, waiting.

Anna nodded. "We figured it out, so we went looking for the painting, and —"

José's mother looked at Aunt Lucinda with daggers in her eyes. "I told you that was a bad idea." She turned back to Anna. "And you looked . . . where?"

"The Catacombs. And we found it," Henry said, "only it turned out to be Brittany instead, and —"

"Hold on . . ." Anna's mom shook her head. "Brittany?"

"That's what we called the painting to keep it a secret," Henry went on. "But we found the decoy. The one that was all rolled up. I snuck it out in my pants."

"Oh, Henry," Aunt Lucinda said.

José's dad swallowed a laugh. "Go on."

"That's when we went into the tunnels and found Hem and Vincent Junior. And then Anna and José went back for the real painting, but I was mad at him" — Henry jerked his thumb toward Hem — "so I went back to the bookstore and . . ." A lump grew in his throat. He swallowed hard. "I told Ursa what was going on. I thought she was on our side." He looked at his dad, eyes burning with tears. "I'm so sorry."

His dad nodded and slid his chair closer so he could put an arm around Henry. "You didn't know. No one did until it was too late. You did your best."

Henry shook his head. "But then I lost the painting, too. I was trying to trade and get you guys back and —"

"Hold on now!" Aunt Lucinda cut him off. "You tried to trade the *Mona Lisa* for us?"

Henry nodded miserably and told them the rest of the story — how he tracked down the real *Mona Lisa* after Anna and José and Hem had hidden it at the souvenir stand, how he'd left the note on the bookstore bulletin board and climbed the cathedral tower and waited in the rain and handed over the *Mona Lisa* and raced down to find everyone thinking that they were free. . . .

"Only I got there and you were gone!" He blinked as fast as he could, but he couldn't keep up with the tears. Their waiter started to swoop in with a pitcher of water, but Henry's blubbering scared him off. "And when I finally found you, it wasn't you at all." Henry shook his head, remembering. "It was this dumb guy in your jacket. And then the painting was gone."

His dad looked at the other grown-ups, shaking his head. Then he looked back at Henry. "And then you tracked us down."

Henry nodded.

"And got us out."

"But I gave them the painting. And society members promise to protect —"

"One another," Aunt Lucinda said quietly. "When we were on missions together years ago, your mom always reminded me that people come first. Art is important, but people come first."

"I know." Henry did know. He couldn't imagine going on if he'd lost his dad or Aunt Lucinda or Anna or José or even Hem. But he wished he could have saved the painting, too. He picked up a piece of bread and pinched it into a tight little ball.

"Henry?" Aunt Lucinda said.

"Yeah?"

"The *Mona Lisa* is safe."

Henry looked up from his bread ball. "They found her?"

Anna's face lit up. "Already? That's amazing! Where was she?"

"She was never lost," Anna's mother said. "The rolled-up painting . . . Brittany? Is that what you called her?" She made a face.

"It made sense at the time," José mumbled.

"Anyway," Anna's mom went on. "That painting was a decoy. And so was the other reproduction that you went back for — an even more authentic-looking version on poplar, just like the original. Both were meant to throw the Serpentine Prince gang off track so they wouldn't go looking for the real painting."

"That's awesome!" Anna pulled her notebook from the backpack Henry had returned to her. "But wait . . . aren't they art experts, too? Wouldn't they have known da Vinci painted the *Mona Lisa* on wood?"

"Goosen is most definitely an expert, and he would have known," Anna's mom said, "but he's too terrified of heights to go down the ladders into those tunnels himself. And the thug criminals he hires for this kind of search job aren't the brightest. They wouldn't have had a clue the rolled-up canvas was a fake. If they'd found it, they'd have taken it to Goosen, and he would have sent them right back down to keep searching. It was all meant to buy us more time."

"So. Cool." Anna scribbled some notes and looked up. "So where's the real one, then?"

"She never left the museum," Aunt Lucinda said

proudly. She looked at Henry. "The painting you lost — the one painted on the wood panel — was done earlier this week by a society member's niece who happens to be a student at the Paris College of Art. She did a fine job, mind you, but she's not quite up there with da Vinci yet."

"Wow. That's pretty awesome." Henry felt warm, like all that cold dampness from the park bushes was finally gone. And just when he thought the night couldn't get better, the waiter showed up with a pot of melted chocolate and strawberries and fluffy cake to dip in it.

Hem reached for a strawberry. Henry raised his eyebrows. "Pretending you're a tourist?"

Hem nodded. "Chocolate is chocolate, mate. And it's always a good way to celebrate."

· • ◎ • ·

There was nothing like having slept in wet mulch under a bush to make a thinly cushioned bookstore bench feel like the most luxurious bed in the universe.

Henry had his duffel bag all packed and was settling in when José, Anna, and Hem came over to his bench by the bulletin board. He scooched over into a corner to make room.

"I guess Joan of Arc came through after all," José said, climbing onto the bench with his quote book in his hand. Hem sprawled out on the other side of the bench. Anna sat down next to him and went back to writing in her notebook.

"Yeah, she was okay. I wonder if it works better if you actually pay for the candle." Henry looked at the quote book. "Sorry if I got that kind of damp. I found some pretty good stuff in there."

José nodded. "It's fine. I spilled lemon-lime soda on it once, so the pages were already a little wavy anyway."

Anna tore a page from her notebook.

"Finish your news story?" Henry asked.

"No. I'm going to be working on that for a while. I'll need to make some calls when I get home, collect quotes, you know." She held up the notebook page. "This is for the wall of fame." She pulled a Band-Aid from the smallest pocket of her backpack, peeled off the back, and bandaged her notebook page to the wall, right where they'd found the orange napkin that started this whole thing. Henry got up on his knees to read it:

Dear Paris, Thanks for the adventure. Some day, I'll be back to work at Connexion. Save some Nutella for me! xoxo Anna Revere-Hobbs

"I think you spelled connection wrong." Henry pointed.

"No, that's how you spell it. It's an English news-paper here. I was talking with one of the reporters at the Interpol news conference, and he said they have internships for college kids. I figure if I study abroad, I'll be perfect. You know, because I already have so much experience here."

Henry nodded. "Three whole days."

"Well, yeah, but they weren't ordinary days. Hey, you guys need to put something up there, too!" She tore some pages from her notebook and passed them out.

José and Hem started scribbling right away.

Henry hated blank pages. They reminded him too much of English class. He tried to draw a *Mona Lisa*, but her smile wasn't right, and instead of long dark hair, she looked like she had a monkey flopped over her head.

Henry leaned over José's paper. "What did you write?"

"Take a guess," José said.

"Some quote, I bet," Henry said. "Shakespeare?"

"Close." José stuck his paper to the wall and moved back so Henry could read.

It is our choices, Harry, that show what we
truly are, far more than our abilities.
— Albus Dumbledore

"He said a lot of great things, but that's my favorite," José said.

Henry nodded and looked at Hem. "Where's yours?"

Hem pointed to the wall, at his map.

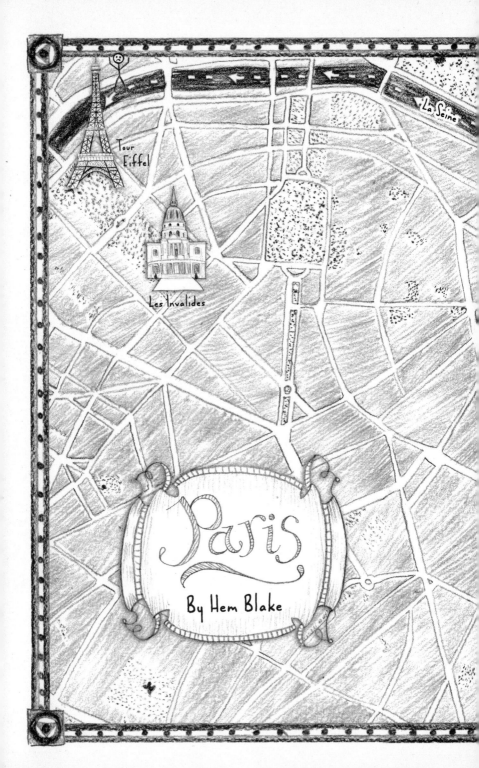

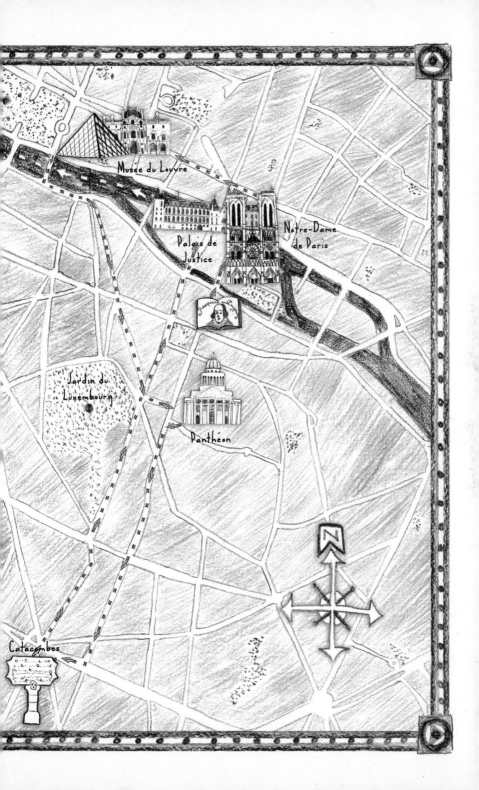

It traced their path from Shakespeare and Company, to Notre-Dame, the Louvre, and the Panthéon, to the Catacombs and the underground tunnels, and finally from the Conciergerie to the Eiffel Tower. Hem had even drawn in a stick figure of Vincent Goosen, scowling in the Seine near the boat.

"Nice." Henry looked back at his own paper. The monkey and *Mona Lisa* looked as if they were waiting for him to write something. But he couldn't think of anything smart enough. He needed better words. "Hey." He tapped José's quote book. "Can I borrow this for a second?"

José nodded, and Henry flipped pages until he came to the quote he was looking for. He knew it, but he wanted to make sure he got it right.

Walk on with hope in your heart, and you'll never walk alone.
— from Carousel

Then he added:

Buy jeans that fit, and you'll never have to hide a painting in your pants.
— Henry Thorn

José nodded. "Good choices."

Henry Band-Aided his paper to the wall, and they all sat for a few minutes, staring up at the quotes and notes and thoughts from people all over the world.

"It's kind of cool to put something up there, you know?" Henry said. "Like we're leaving but not totally."

"You never really leave Paris," Hem said. "Once you've seen the Eiffel Tower at night, a part of you stays behind in the reflection of the Seine." He looked at Anna and José and Henry. "That's so you'll have to come back to visit. You have no choice, really," he said.

Anna ran her hand lightly over the board, ruffling the edges of a dozen notes. "I bet all these people think they'll be back some day."

José stared up at the board. "All these people from all over the world — people we'll never meet — knelt on this same bench and stuck their words to the wall like us. And now we're all kind of connected, don't you think?"

"Yeah." A few days ago, Henry would have thought that was dumb, and he sure wouldn't have wanted to be connected to Hem. But now . . . it really did feel that way. "I hope —" He stopped himself because he didn't want it to come out wrong. "It's not like I hope art gets stolen, but . . . well, now that Goosen's locked up, I hope I still get to see you guys."

"I know." Anna looked down and twisted her notebook rings. "I thought about that, too. Stopping the Serpentine Prince gang was such a huge part of the society's work. What if . . ."

Hem's laugh interrupted her. "You do realize that Vincent Goosen isn't even fifty years old, yes?"

"What does that have to do with it?" Anna asked.

"Everything." José smiled. "The society's been around for hundreds of years, Anna. It was alive before Vincent Goosen, and it'll go on after he's gone."

She nodded. "Of course. I just hope I'll see you guys soon."

"Me too," Henry said. He had a feeling he would. Then he yawned. "But right now, I kind of wish you'd get off my bed so I could go to sleep."

José and Anna and Hem laughed and left Henry to his bench. He plugged in his SuperGamePrism, then stretched out and pulled up his flimsy blanket and looked up at the rough paper corners sticking out from the wall of fame, words full of so many people's promises and hopes.

Henry felt connected to all of them — to all the Post-it note scribblers, to Anna and José and Hem, too. And he knew he'd still feel that way when he was back on his own side of the ocean. Even when he said good-bye to Anna and José, they'd be connected, and it would be okay.

Finally, he closed his eyes and thought about getting on that plane tomorrow, flying away from Paris and its twinkling tower, toward his next adventure. He had a baby sister to meet.

AUTHOR'S NOTE

Whenever I visit schools and libraries to talk about the Silver Jaguar Society mysteries, the first questions I get asked are about the society itself. . . .

"Is the Silver Jaguar Society real? And are you a member?"

My answers to those questions? "No . . ." and "I wish."

But while the Silver Jaguar Society and the group's archenemies, the Serpentine Prince gang, are fictional, many other places and groups in *Manhunt* are real. While I was researching and brainstorming this mystery, my family and I spent time in both Boston and Paris, in many of the settings that Henry, Anna, and José explore in the book.

The Isabella Stewart Gardner Museum is a real art museum in Boston, and the story about thieves breaking in to slice paintings from their canvases in 1990 is true. Those paintings included works by Rembrandt and Vermeer, but the John Singer Sargent portrait of Mrs. Gardner herself remained safe and sound in its spot on the wall. The stolen paintings from the 1990 heist have not yet been recovered, though the FBI now says it believes an organized crime group was responsible.

The Old North Church is also a real place in Boston, with a real crypt (and real human remains!) beneath it.

The tour guide's stories about stolen angels in the choir loft and historic Boston tunnels used by pirates and smugglers are also real historical details. Most, if not all those tunnels, have now been sealed, but our guide at the Old North Church told us a story about some teenagers who broke into one some years ago, went exploring, and ultimately found themselves in the basement of the church gift shop, along with all those boxes of souvenirs and T-shirts.

In Paris, the famous Notre-Dame Cathedral really does have a dusty underground crypt and a grand rooftop guarded by great stone gargoyles and chimera. This one, which Henry thought looked bored with the view, was my favorite.

The basement of the Musée du Louvre does indeed show off the remains of the original palace, including the dungeon. I spent an evening at the Louvre, walking around the circular path with my notebook until I found a suitable place for Hem to hide.

The Panthéon really is where some of France's most distinguished citizens are buried, and the Foucault's pendulum in its great hall is every bit as mesmerizing as Henry, Anna, and José found it in the book.

Although the Silver Jaguar Society is a product of my imagination, I'm delighted to tell you that another secret society mentioned in the book — the UX — is real, and its members did indeed break into the Panthéon to restore its clock. You can read more

about that in this newspaper article from the *Guardian*:
http://www.guardian.co.uk/world/2007/nov/26/france.artnews

The Conciergerie is another real historical site, though to the best of my knowledge, it has not been infiltrated by bad guys. (I made that part up.) Once a royal palace, it was used as a prison during the French Revolution and is now a museum. Some of the cells remain, along with a glass case full of big old keys. No one broke it with a ladder while I was there.

The most chilling and most fascinating part of my Paris research trip was my visit to the Catacombs — tunnels full of bones that are every bit as creepy and claustrophobic as Henry describes them.

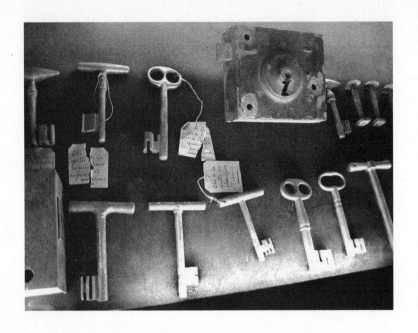

The one place I did not visit in person was the domain of the cataphiles — those off-limits underground tunnels that used to be part of the city's quarries. For safety reasons — and because I like to avoid being arrested when I'm traveling — I relied on books, Internet research, photographs, and videos for these scenes. Before I went to Paris, I'd tried — with no luck — to find a real-life cataphile to interview about the underground world, but it wasn't until my last day in the city that I found the right person. I'd just climbed the winding stairs up from the Catacombs and wandered into a nearby gift shop to look at some books. One of them had stunning photographs of those secret underground tunnels, and when the

Ils furent ce que nous sommes,
Poussière, jouet du vent;
Fragiles comme des hommes,
Faibles comme le néant!

LAMARTINE

young man behind the register saw me looking at them, he came over to pick up yet another book full of amazing photos.

"You must see this one," he said, turning to a picture that showed a flooded tunnel, reflecting some kind of magical blue-white light from above.

"That's amazing," I said.

"And you wouldn't believe how perfectly quiet it is . . . just the sound of your footsteps and the water dripping." He sighed, and I knew I'd found one of those people Hem described, Paris rebels who somehow feel most at home underground.

"You've been there, haven't you?"

He grinned. "Perhaps a time or two." He kindly spent the better part of an hour answering questions as I scribbled furiously in my notebook, and finally, he sent us off with directions to a manhole cover not far away, where we could see what one of the access points looked like. It was nondescript metal circle in the sidewalk, well-sealed, with not a crowbar in sight, but I could imagine what it would be like to pry off that cover, climb down a rusty ladder, and descend into the shadowy, damp world below.

Finally, I'm happy to report that the bookstore Shakespeare and Company is a very real place on Paris's Left Bank.

It really is a home away from home for writers who need a place to stay in Paris. They sleep on benches

right in the store, just like Henry, Anna, and José. In the children's section, there really is a bulletin board where messages spill onto the walls and ceiling, affixed with everything from paper clips to Band-Aids. Many of the personal notes that Anna, Henry, and José notice are notes that I saw on the wall during my visit.

I didn't find any secret society missives on the board. But like Henry, Anna, and José, I did leave a note of my own, and I hope to return some day, too.

ABOUT THE AUTHOR

KATE MESSNER is the author of *The Brilliant Fall of Gianna Z.*, winner of the E. B. White Read Aloud Award for Older Readers; *Capture the Flag*, an SCBWI Crystal Kite Award winner; *Over and Under the Snow*, a *New York Times* Notable Children's Book; the Marty McGuire chapter book series; and several other books for young readers. A former middle-school English teacher, Kate lives on Lake Champlain with her family and loves reading, walking in the woods, and traveling. Visit her online at www.katemessner.com.